DEATH O

Bodie belted through the outer door, took it all in, saw that shadowed form with the upraised pistol, and triggered two quick shots from his Browning.

The slugs hit O'Leary in the chest, driving him back. He swivelled sideways, collapsing, clawing desperately and sending the sheets of manuscript billowing up into the room.

Bodie roared in, ready to shoot again and keep on shooting for as long as was necessary.

Doyle leaped up and followed him in.

O'Leary tried to rise, tried to stand – but his legs buckled. He coughed bright red. He fell down and rolled, his arm flopped out limply, and he was dead.

Also by Ken Blake in Sphere Books:

THE PROFESSIONALS 1: WHERE THE JUNGLE ENDS
THE PROFESSIONALS 2: LONG SHOT
THE PROFESSIONALS 3: STAKE OUT
THE PROFESSIONALS 4: HUNTER HUNTED
THE PROFESSIONALS 5: BLIND RUN

THE PROFESSIONALS:
Fall Girl

KEN BLAKE

Based on the original screenplays by
Ronald Graham, Edmund Ward and Don Houghton

SPHERE BOOKS LIMITED
30/32 Gray's Inn Road, London WCIX 8JL

First published by Sphere Books Ltd 1979

TRADE
MARK

Set in Intertype Baskerville

Printed in Great Britain by
Hunt Barnard Printing Ltd,
Aylesbury, Bucks.

Chapter One

Bodie's silver-grey Capri tooled easily through thickening London traffic. The weather looked promising for the week-end and once they were out of the congested inner streets and free of the rush he'd let her rip. At his side Doyle yawned and then reached up to the radio telephone neatly concealed behind the sun visor.

Letting the Capri drift along the street in the traffic flow past tall office blocks, expensive shops and the passing crowds, Bodie glanced at his partner and away. The International Hotel showed up ahead, its canopy of glass and steel just visible over the car roofs. Sunshine picked out the glitter of plush living.

Doyle spoke easily into the microphone.

'4.5 and 3.7 signing off, over.'

From the communications centre of C.I.5 H.Q. in its anonymous and drab building just off Whitehall Julia's voice reached into the Capri.

'4.5 and 3.7. O.K. You are clear. Have a good week-end.'

'And you too, darling,' said Doyle, with one of his wide happy smiles. 'Over and out.'

He flicked off the R./T. and settled back in his seat, low and comfortable.

The cars moved on again and Bodie let the Capri pick up speed. The bottleneck up ahead cleared and the traffic flow resumed normal pace. Doyle's smile remained.

'Mmmh!' he said with a little shiver of anticipation. 'Saturday . . . Sunday . . . Funny, you take two days off in the middle of the week and it's never the same.' His tousled head leaned back and his smile became positively dreamy. He kissed his fingers, an extravagant gesture that evocatively summed up the goodness he felt for life. His round pugnacious face relaxed. 'Le – week-end!' he said in a French accent.

Bodie's face did not relax in quite the same way. But he gave that little idiosyncratic twist of his head that in a strange way revealed instantly his awareness of what was going through his partner's mind. Very handsome, very debonair, very much the man of the world, Bodie, and highly lethal with it.

'You,' he said strictly to Doyle, 'have been taking French lessons.'

'Those,' said Doyle, 'I give!'

Doyle pushed in a cassette and some light frothy popular music filled the interior of the Capri half-drowning the mumble of engines.

Onlookers gathered on the pavement outside the Hotel International as the imposing black limousine glided in to the kerb. Press photographers pushed to get their sights aligned on the door of the limousine, ready for the very first glimpse of Marikka Schumann. She was everything that a glamour-hungry public wanted. A famous East German film actress, beautiful in a dark impish way, slender, elegant, giving off that special aura of allure – you'd say she was a ballet dancer by the way she moved. And the fact that she was East German lent her an air of mystery and exotic fascination that no Hollywood or everyday TV star could command, or so it was said.

It was said very loudly by Kurt Kreiber, the East German Public Relations official, who handled the photographers very well. Now he stood waiting for the limousine, holding the bunch of flowers, remembering to smile, waiting for Marikka.

A smooth man, Kreiber, sleek and dark, with rat-trap jaws that revealed more of his ruthless nature than he would perhaps have cared for, had he realised his inner nature could be penetrated. A dangerous man, Kreiber, and yet here he was, smiling, confident, radiating charm, and holding a bunch of flowers in the sunshine.

The big shining limousine pulled up and even as the uniformed chauffeur leaped out, the uniformed hotel doorman pounced forward to open the door with a flourish. Everyone was anxious to help Marikka and, whilst they were doing that, stand close to her and gaze at her. Kreiber and his flowers advanced, beaming.

Marikka stepped down. The crowd ogled. She glanced about, perfectly composed, assured, smiling with that distant smile of the professional which she infused with that special brand of her own glamorous magic. Her husband, Max Schumann, followed her out of the limousine and as Kreiber presented his bouquet of flowers, so Schumann put his arm protectively around the slender shoulders of his wife.

The gesture might have been construed as charming, showing the care and concern of a film producer husband for his film star wife. Yet to some of the onlookers there was much about that gesture that said: this woman is mine – hands off.

Max Schumann held on to Marikka as the photographs were taken and the flash bulbs dazzled. A strong-looking man, intent, quiffed of hair and pugnacious of face, he looked to be the kind of man who ruled the roost.

A girl with long hair and a C&A coat pushed up eagerly proffering her autograph book. Smiling happily, Marikka took the book and accepted the ballpoint and began to sign.

She underlined her name with a flourish and looked up.

She saw a silver-grey car, trapped by the traffic, just easing past the Hotel International. Two men sat in the car and one of them – his hair looked like a tousled bearskin through the window – was looking away. But the one driving – Marikka looked straight at him. She saw his face – that face! She saw the lean strength there, the dark impeccable coiffed hair, the quizzical look. She gaped.

The Capri swerved.

The car leaped ahead towards the crossroads ignoring crossing traffic. Doyle lurched against his seat.

'Watch out!' he yelled.

The Vauxhall sedately crossing ahead of them swerved one way and as Bodie sawed the wheel the Capri swerved the other way. A honking of car horns began, stridently, and Bodie, thin-lipped, hauled his car straight and punched ahead, his eyes fixed, glaring at the road.

'What's the matter with you? You trying to kill us?'

Bodie licked his lips. He gave a little shake of his head and did not answer.

Outside the Hotel International Schumann had both arms around Marikka now, staring at her with concern. The press photographers clicked away.

'Are you all right?'

She did not answer at once, and Kreiber hovered, trying to take the bouquet away; but Marikka clung on to the flowers like a drowning person holds on to the lifebelt. She swallowed down. She made herself remember where she was and who she was. With an effort she pulled herself together. She smiled.

That smile reassured almost everyone.

'I'm quite all right. The drive from the airport . . .'

'Car sick,' nodded Kreiber. At once he began to exert himself and ushered the group through into the foyer. The photographers packed up and the crowd, chattering, drifted away.

The pub was that quiet relaxing kind of establishment where discreet service included all you could pay for. Doyle and Bodie sat on the terrace outside with the old beams and ancient brickwork framing the latticed windows. The tables were spikey white-painted iron. The seats were the same, too, but they possessed cushions and were, all in all, quite comfortable. A few coloured umbrellas supported on poles rising from holes at the centres of the tables added the nice touch of holiday both agents craved. Doyle, who had set up the arrangements to meet the girls tonight, came out of the pub. He held the remains of a pint. His face was decidedly irritable.

'That guy's still using the phone,' he said, disgruntled. He flopped down at the table where Bodie sat. Bodie's face was set into lines that Doyle, annoyed at the way the time was slipping away, took in only half-aware. He looked at his watch.

'We're going to miss them at this rate.'

He got up again and went to the door of the pub. The sounds of laughter from the other tables made Bodie stir not a hair. He sat, half-slumped, clutching his drink, his thoughts miles away. At his feet the tennis bags lay, a little forlornly, matching the holiday attire of Bodie with his preoccupied air.

Doyle came back to the table, thoroughly fed-up, making up his mind. 'Give me some cover.'

Bodie looked about, reached across to the next table, which was unoccupied, and picked up the *Guardian*. He shook it out, partially shielding Doyle. Doyle took out his walkie-talkie, a miniaturised model, and bent his head to it. He looked very suspicious. Bodie shook the paper out a little more.

Doyle, in a soft breathy voice, said: '4.5 to Base. Julia – Doyle here. Listen, sweetheart, I have a grade zero emergency. Could you call this number for me – three seven eight four six nine two – ' He took a breath and cowered even more behind Bodie's borrowed newspaper. 'Tell Christine to call her friend, and for them both to meet us at Dino's wine bar – seven-thirty . . .'

'This,' Julia's voice said with the suspicion of a sniff, 'is strictly against regulations.'

Doyle winked at Bodie. 'I'll make it up to you.'

'You're all mouth and trousers, 4.5!'

'You better be careful.' Doyle relaxed, knowing that Julia would relay the message. 'I'm licensed to thrill.'

'Ha, ha. I'll call you back.'

'Wait. That message is for Christine. If a man answers, you're a girl friend of Christine's, right . . . ?'

'I don't think I'd like her – '

'You're right.' Now Doyle smiled. 'I don't think you would.'

Doyle finished with the walkie-talkie and turned to Bodie whose face was now hidden by the paper.

'You know, Bodie, that Julia – she's interesting.' He waited and got no reaction. 'You think?'

Still Bodie made no reply.

'Hey! I don't need the cover any more.'

But Bodie was staring at the paper, staring at a photograph of a beautiful woman, smiling for the cameras, holding a bouquet of flowers. The screamer said: 'East German star visits London.'

That was all that Bodie needed. He hadn't been sure – not really sure – and now he knew. His mouth went dry. He stared at the photograph of Marikka.

Doyle tried again. 'Is there an up-market page three?'

Slowly, so slowly the paper only squeaked instead of rustling, Bodie folded the *Guardian*. He looked blanked out, shocked.

'What?'

'All the nudes that's fit to print?'

Vacantly, his hand still crushing the paper, Bodie said: 'Page three . . . ?'

Doyle heaved up a theatrical smile and thought about the second drink. 'Forget it,' he said. He spoke lightly.

But those two words seemed to echo and crescendo in Bodie's mind. 'Forget it . . . Forget it . . . ' The words whirled into him and through him, and he knew he wouldn't – he couldn't . . .

So it was her . . . That single swift glimpse from the car as they'd passed the Hotel International had seemed to

Bodie then to drag up a memory and then to lay it . . . And now, here it was again. He hesitated outside the hotel, not even wondering what Ray Doyle was thinking about his disappearance from the holiday pub. In there . . . Marikka . . .

Inside at the bar he took a quick look around, taking in the discreet luxury, ordering a drink, acting casually in the rose and purple lighting. Marikka sat with two men at a table over by the far wall, their hair highlighted by the wall lamps. She saw him. He knew that instantly. Casually, Marikka excused herself and wandered across to the bar, well away from Bodie.

'Could you tell me where the ladies' room is, please?' she said to the barman in that voice Bodie recalled so clearly.

The barman told her and then she said: 'Tell me, if somebody leaves a telephone number with you – could you give it to me – discreetly?'

'A pleasure.' The barman understood all this, understood it very well.

Marikka smiled graciously and went away and Bodie, leaning forward, pushed his glass across the counter. The barman raised his eyebrows in acknowledgement – or, perhaps, as Bodie saw at once – because he was ahead of Bodie. Bodie looked at him calmly, and gave him the phone number. As the barman pushed the refilled glass back, Bodie repeated the number.

'I'll pass it on, sir.'

'Thank you.'

Kurt Kreiber, watching Marikka, saw the brief conversation, saw the man at the bar, recognised something in him, some lean feral strength he could comprehend, and he spoke to Max Schumann. Schumann looked across at Bodie. His eyes were cold and hard.

Finishing his drink, Bodie took off. He hadn't believed it, still didn't believe anything would come of it – but then he remembered Marikka, and felt that tingle along his spine. If she wanted to, she would arrange a meet. He went back to the holiday pub and the wrath of his partner.

'So,' said Doyle. 'What happened to you last night?'

'No excuse.'

'No excuse! That's not an excuse.' Doyle was, as Bodie saw quickly enough, not so much annoyed as inquisitive. 'Anyway, you missed out in a big way, my friend.'

'Oh, yes?'

Doyle shook his head. 'Frankie – Christine's friend – well, her hobby . . . ' He stopped himself, looked hard at Bodie, and said quickly: 'Where *were* you Saturday night?'

'An urgent meeting with my psychiatrist.'

The barmaid walked up then, not too displeased to have an excuse to tangle again with these two quick-tongued romeos, and told Bodie a phone call waited for him. He felt the sharp stab take him, and stood up, not looking at Doyle.

'Thanks, princess.'

'You call me that again,' said the barmaid, an ample girl with nice hair and lips but whose teeth lacked a certain something, 'and I'll crown you!'

Bodie blew her a kiss and walked off to the phone. The barmaid winked at Doyle, and then, recovering herself, went away quickly. These supercharged romeos could get her going, and no mistake.

The man on the line said: 'Mr Bodie? My name is Kurt Kreiber. I handle publicity for Marikka Schumann.' In the slight pause Bodie did not bite; he remained listening, face composed. 'Marikka wishes to get in touch with you. But it is very difficult, you understand. However, she has asked me to arrange it – with you – she has so many receptions and functions it is impossible for her to get much time.'

'I'd like to talk to her – even on the phone.'

'Look. She is now at a screening of her latest film, out at the Leyton Studios. Just down the road from there is a service station. Know it?'

'Yes.'

'Meet me in the rest area, there's a kind of arcade, and I will try to arrange something between now and then.'

'How do I recognise you?'

'I shall be wearing a bow tie and I have a – uh – a

herringbone jacket. Sort of blue. Dark blue.'

'I'll be there.'

Replacing the receiver, Bodie felt the most curious sensation grip him; he felt at once nervous and excited. Nervous? A tough, calloused, hard-bitten agent of C.I.5, the Action Squad, the Big A – nervous? He pulled his jacket straight and went out to persuade Doyle to drive.

By this time in their relationship, Doyle knew there were depths to Bodie that he had not plumbed – not so far. Intrigued by his partner's evident hyped state, Doyle drove his white Escort out to the service station and dropped Bodie.

'Where you going from here?'

Bodie eyed him. His lips crinkled up in that famous Bodie crinkle; he made up his mind.

'Doyle – I got a meet – strictly social.'

Doyle looked at once annoyed and understanding. 'O.K., O.K. Listen. What am I going to do about these two girls?'

'I'll call you later.'

'We'll be in Dino's wine bar until eight.' Doyle made his round pugnacious face look threatening. 'If you're not there by then, I'll formally announce my *ménage à trois*.'

Bodie merely nodded, thus depriving Doyle of the suitable rejoinder he had ready to cap Bodie's expected sarcasm. Bodie walked off. Fed up, Doyle checked his petrol gauge and reasoned that as Mohammed had come to the mountain, as it were, he might as well fill the tank whilst he was here. He tooled the white Escort along towards the pumps.

Bodie entered the arcade warily, immediately surrounded by flashing lights and ringing bells and the clickety-clack of little balls spinning and spitting in the pin-ball machines. He spotted the man who fitted the description he'd been given over by a test-your-shooting-skill machine. He had a rifle butt tucked into his shoulder and was blasting away at the targets. There was an ominous absence of cheery rings denoting hits from the bowels of the machine. Bodie sauntered over.

'Mr Kreiber?'

Kreiber just then scored a hit and the brittle ring enthused him. 'Wait – I'm going for a record.' He pressed the trigger. 'Damn – missed!' Then the bell ding-donged splendidly. 'Hah! Two more shots!' He fired twice and then stepped back disgustedly. The rifle butt dangled. He shook his head and glared at the machine as though it had charged him income tax.

'Every time, I miss that last one.'

He fished in his pocket for more change.

Kreiber glanced at Bodie, who just stood waiting for the pantomime to finish. This wasn't what he'd come for.

'It's not so easy,' said Kreiber. 'You must try – '

'Look – ' Bodie felt his patience shredding like salt in a hurricane.

'Mr Bodie.' There was a trace of snappiness in Kreiber's voice. 'You are causing me a lot of trouble. My job is to keep things smooth and shipshape. Actresses are enough of a handful at the best of times. But when they start having problems of the heart . . . '

Bodie looked about, taking in what the P.R. man said.

'Is she coming here now?'

Kreiber delicately but firmly indicated that Bodie should play the machine. That made sense to Bodie, trained to fade into the background. He snugged the rifle butt into his shoulder. Thc rifle was just a butt; all the rest was mirrors and electronic gadgetry.

'I have arranged a meeting for Marikka and you. We must be careful about her husband. He is – a little – jealous.'

By the time Doyle had filled the tank and was driving back past the rest area and the arcade he was in a good position to observe Bodie talking to a dark and very smooth-looking man as they walked towards the exit. Puzzled, Doyle watched them leave. A couple of mechanics in soiled smocks went to the rifle shooting machine. Doyle saw them and then figuring his interest lay with Bodie and not a couple of fellows repairing busted games, he drove on.

The two men at the rifle butt produced their toolkits and started in on their maintenance job.

The quiet easiness of the evening with shadows lengthening across the grass soft and dreamy-edged, with the leaves of trees motionless, a gentle balm in the air and a yearning sense of time stretching out and yet held and contained in these last evening moments seemed to Bodie the most perfect time to meet Marikka again. They saw each other a long way off in the park, under the trees, two tiny figures in a mild landscape of mellowness, and there was, suddenly, no need to hurry.

Slowly they walked towards each other, savouring the full meaning of these moments. This was a time to cherish, these few heartbeats before they met, at last, and again.

They halted and stood, looking at each other, a little way still apart.

'Hello.'

'Bodie ...'

For what seemed a long time they looked at each other, examining the tricks that the years had played on them, remembering. Marikka was still lovely. Bodie was still handsome.

'You haven't changed.'

'Neither have you.'

They spoke quietly and calmly, with pauses in which they contemplated the other, half-smiling, serious, savouring every moment.

'How long are you here for?'

'Three more days.'

'It said in the paper – your husband ...'

'Yes. He's produced all my films.'

'That's why you married him?' Bodie looked away and the furrow appeared between his eyebrows. 'Sorry.'

'Max is a very strange man. He has done everything for me. Yet I know, if ever I became a problem for him, he would ditch me. Just like that.' Her face remained calm, revealing in no way the terrible inner meaning of her words.

'You know what our country is like. Everything is so – so political.' She tossed her head back and the declining sunlight caught a radiance in her face. 'And you – what about yourself? Are you still fighting in all those obscure wars that never get mentioned in the newspapers – where were they, Africa, the Middle East . . . ?'

'I've stopped all that.'

'What do you do now?'

Bodie wanted to – he wasn't completely sure what he wanted to do beyond this moment. 'A job.'

'You don't want to talk about it?'

Bodie said, 'What sort of films do you make?'

Marikka tossed her head again, and shed some of that inner sense of foreboding, that inner sense of desolation. 'They're terrible!' She made a face and struck a half-hearted pose of Garbo in anguish. 'Sweetheart. Our love for our country is more important than our love for each other!'

Bodie crinkled up his eyebrows. Obtusely, he said: 'What does that mean?'

In a reasonable, explaining voice, Marikka told him: 'Sweetheart. Our love for our country is more important than our love for each other.'

'You believe that stuff?'

'You know – I don't know any longer. The older I get, the less I seem to understand anything.' She stared levelly at Bodie. 'You! You used to be so sure, so strong, about everything.'

'Even about you.'

Marikka took his arm and they began to walk, slowly, side by side. The physical contact warmed Bodie. The park lay about them, golden and mellow, with the shadows lying on the grass.

'Bodie . . . What could *we* have done together . . .'

'We had some good times.'

'They were great times.' She looked up at him, and smiled. 'The most wonderful of my life.'

After a long pause, Bodie said: 'Are you happy?'

She squeezed his hand. 'I don't know.'

'If you don't know – then you're not.'

Marikka shook her head, disorientated for a moment. Then: 'I disagree.' She looked away. 'I think.'

They reached the pond and stood looking at the ducks who were methodically and carefully preparing for the night. The white and brown feathers blended with the stillness of the shadowed water. The air hung, still and close and yet with that indefinable evening tang, not chill yet carrying the outdoors to their senses.

'Stand still, for a moment.' Bodie gently put his hand up to Marikka's hair, looked behind her ear.

'My mole?'

'It's still there –'

'Where could it have gone?' Marikka laughed, delighted at the foolishness.

Soberly, Bodie said: 'I don't know. It's been in my head for a long time.'

As though signalled by a yearning neither could comprehend and yet understood all too well, Bodie, turning her around, kissed her lightly. She shivered. They kissed more passionately until Marikka, gasping, broke away. She turned her back on him.

'No, Bodie.'

She half-turned and Bodie saw the tears standing in her eyes, large and glistening and yet still unshed. He took a breath.

Marikka reached out her hand.

'Come on! Walk with me for a little.'

They walked towards the wrought-iron railings and found a gate, the iron gilded in spear-points, and went out on to the pavement where the traffic roared on past, uncaring, blue exhaust fumes destroying the lingering evening in the park.

'I'll call you – please.' Marikka pleaded. 'I must go now. I'm already late.'

'You'll call. You promise?'

'I promise.'

They looked at each other. Then, slowly, they kissed, warmly and gently, understandingly.

Bodie brisked himself up as the traffic roar broke into ugly noises aimed directly, it seemed, at him personally. He smiled, wondering if she would call. He took her arm and steered her along the pavement. 'Come on. Your sauerkraut is getting cold.'

She did not surprise him as she gave him a hefty but friendly thump of rebuke with her free hand on his back. He'd known Marikka, in the old days . . .

They reached the edge of the pavement, their backs to the gilded park railings, facing the roaring tide of traffic.

'I must walk to the hotel from here by myself.'

Bodie had to act it up. 'I wouldn't dare be seen with you!'

She lifted on tip-toes to give him a quick, moist kiss, then hurried away. Bodie stood, watching her, seeing the way she walked, the litheness of it, the movements of her body, thinking. She had said those days had been the happiest of her life. They had been good, sweet and tender and brief. And now everything was different, and she was married and a famous film star and he was an agent for the Big A, the squad dedicated to fighting crime with its own weapons, dirty or not. He watched Marikka as she walked away among the people, out of his sight, and he wondered if she would call.

In the car parked a little way along, the camera with its infra-red telephoto lens, which had been greedily sucking in picture after picture of Bodie and Marikka, took its last quick flash of his face, thoughtful, partially illuminated by the first of the park lamps, contemplating thoughts the camera could never guess – and, perhaps, Bodie's face was a little resigned. Fate had dealt to him off the bottom of the deck enough times in his hectic life for the experience to be no novelty.

Colour and brightness filled St James's Park with the sense of a happily-used garden in the midst of a hustling city.

George Cowley walked with Willis along the gravel ways, deep in conversation. This park had probably been used for so many high-powered and secret conversations that if the trees had ears they'd have made a fortune on the markets of various nations' apparats. And George Cowley was walking. The head of C.I.5 with a damned bullet in his leg felt the litheness there this morning, the freedom and wonderful absence of pain, and he walked along briskly. What he was listening to took a lot, took a very great deal, out of his enjoyment of the park and the sunshine and the walk.

Willis was the head of a security organisation with certain responsibilities that – now – were no concern of Cowley's. Willis had a peanut-shaped head, and black hair slicked down like a wet otter's. He handed Cowley a set of photographs. They showed, grainy but clear, Bodie and the East German film star, Marikka Schumann.

'She's Schumann's wife,' observed Willis, striding on in his immaculate dark-grey suit, master of the situation he was creating.

'But,' said Cowley. 'Does she know about her husband's other activities?'

'You mean, is she a spy, too?' He flicked his cane at the leaves. 'It's a strong possibility.'

Cowley looked at the photographs again. Sandy haired, lined of face, craggy good looks still in evidence, George Cowley was hell-on-wheels when it came to anyone – anyone – letting down the Big A, the Action Squad, the force he had set up to a Government brief to combat crime. Willis went on speaking.

'I'm afraid your man is now under official surveillance by my department. This means, of course, that you yourself are forbidden to communicate this fact to him. And, needless to say, he cannot receive any assignments from you until he is cleared.'

Cowley did not relish this, although he would be the first to acknowledge its practicality, not to say its necessity in security work. Willis took the photographs back.

'What Schumann is up to at this time we have no idea.

There is even the possibility that the woman herself is an agent. We'll find out; but the intrigue level is pretty high. Your boy is way out of his depth.'

Cowley said flatly: 'My boy – ' He emphasised the word with some irony for Willis. 'My boy does not like being followed. Your men had better be careful.'

'They can handle themselves.'

Willis took himself off, sleek, jaunty, swinging his cane.

Cowley stared after him. Softly, he said: 'So can he!'

If Bodie was struck by his association with this woman from any investigation, the only thing Cowley could do was call in Ray Doyle. Something about the set-up made Cowley go around to Doyle's flat instead of handling this in the office. Doyle had just moved into a new pad and the place was in an uproar, filled with packing cases and crates and great piles of crumpled newspapers. Doyle answered the door and looked suitably amazed. Cowley glanced about at the shambles, at the curtainless windows, the dustpan and brush in the corner. Doyle brisked up a half-smile.

'Drink, sir?'

'Yes. Perhaps I will.' Cowley spoke with a weariness that surprised Doyle anew. He looked at the chief, waiting. 'You wouldn't have a small malt?'

Among all the packing cases Doyle knew which was the one. He reached in and produced the bottle, dark and promising potent magics. Cowley stared, pleased. 'Good lad!'

When the drinks had been poured and Cowley sat in a chair with Doyle perched on a packing crate, the bottle to hand, both men were well aware that they had to come to the nub of this unexpected visit. At last Cowley opened with a tentative: 'Have you been seeing much of Bodie, socially, these days?'

Doyle's mobile mouth indicated a private thought: 'He's not my idea of a date.'

'Is he still seeing that Welsh schoolteacher?'

Doyle lowered his glass, baffled. 'What Welsh schoolteacher?' This was a new one to him.

Cowley did not reply directly, finished his drink and Doyle refilled. Cowley stood up and walked to the window – and he limped, he damned well limped. The bullet in his leg started to give him gyp. He spoke in his gravelly voice that all the full plumminess could only partially soften. 'Bodie had a secret meeting with a suspected East German agent.' He swung about and studied Doyle, whose face remained blank. Well, Doyle was a Professional, too . . . 'Willis's man had the suspect under observation. That's how we know. I've seen the photographs.'

'When was this meeting?'

'Last night. I want you to keep an eye on him.'

Everything that C.I.5 meant to the men making up the squad lay revealed in those simple words. Squad and bureaus and organisations were merely formless monsters; it was the men and the women who *were* the squads that counted. Well, sometimes. Sometimes the welfare of the squad was put first. Sometimes . . .

'That'll be hard.'

'It'll be harder.' Cowley lifted his glass but did not drink. 'Willis has him under total surveillance.'

Doyle gave the situation an intuitive thought. 'They'll be watching him, not me.'

Cowley nodded. 'Report in as from now, on Alpha Charlie frequency. All communication from you will be recorded, whether I'm speaking with you or not.'

'When do I start?'

'Immediately.'

Solemnly, Doyle poured his untouched drink back into the bottle. 'I'll need a photograph of this agent.'

Cowley handed across the paper with the picture – the same shot Bodie had reacted to at the holiday pub. 'It's not a him, it's a her.'

Looking at the photograph, seeing through the blotchy black and white grainy newsprint picture something of the beauty and allure of this woman, Doyle pursed his lips.

'You have to hand it to the lad. If he went to the electric chair Miss Universe would throw the switch.'

Quite a number of the Professionals of C.I.5 used the Ivy Bush mainly because the beer was good and the barmaid attractive enough for her sauciness to spice up a dismal lunch hour. Doyle found Bodie there, propping up the bar. Bodie regarded his partner with a distant and mocking look Doyle knew of old.

'Well, how was the *ménage à trois*?'

'At three o'clock this morning,' Doyle said. 'We all decided to fly to Las Vegas and get married.'

'You're back early.'

'At three-fifteen this morning Frankie fell off the table while performing a short excerpt from *Swan Lake*. Sprained a wing.'

'Sounds like a quiet evening.'

'It had its moments.' Doyle surreptitiously wiggled the front of his shirt where the hidden mike nestled, all mixed up with the hairs on his chest. They were listening to everything that was said, back there in C.I.5 communications. 'How was yours?'

Waiting for a reply which would be recorded and might later form the basis of serious charges, Doyle and Bodie were interrupted by the barmaid who cut in to say Bodie had a phone call. He smiled and went off to the booth. Doyle spoke very softly so the mike would pick it up. 'Saved by the bell.'

Doyle drifted across casually as Bodie took his call.

Bodie gripped the receiver and felt the thump along his veins as Marikka's voice whispered in his ear. After a few trivial pleasantries, she said: 'Bodie. I've just done something wicked.'

'What have you done?'

'I've booked two adjoining rooms for us in the hotel opposite, for this afternoon . . . Like the old days . . . '

'I thought you had a reception for Biermann or something.'

'My husband is throwing a long luncheon for some people from the Embassy. It will be awful. I've managed to get out of it. Well?'

'You're right.' Bodie took a breath. 'You are wicked.'

There was no mistaking the tone of Marikka's voice. She was flattered. 'Am I? Really?'

Lovingly, Bodie said, lingering on the word: 'Evil . . .'

'Two o'clock,' Marikka said. 'See you then.'

Bodie put the phone down. He could feel the old trembles shooting through him. They *had* been good days with Marikka.

There was just time to organise things and he left after a few words with Doyle. The sunshine felt good. The day was marvellous. Everybody looked happy. Staring after his partner as Bodie drove off, Doyle reported in through the neck mike and then prepared himself for the tricky business of keeping a tail on Bodie. He had the odd idea that Bodie was so elevated he wouldn't notice if a three-ring circus was following him about. In their profession, that was a highly dangerous state to allow yourself to fall into – dangerous and lethal.

The hotel to which Doyle followed Bodie was smooth, luxurious, glossy and yet holding that distant air of facelessness as though accustomed to the passing trade. The decor, all gold and orange, both invited and yet left unsatisfied. Watching his partner, Doyle saw him hesitate in the parked car, then he bent below the level of the window.

In his Capri, Bodie ditched his I.D., his holstered Browning Auto and his walkie-talkie. He placed them in the glove compartment and locked it, a tight squeeze. Then he got out and went firmly towards the hotel.

Into his mike, Doyle said: 'If he's under surveillance by anyone else they must be doing it by satellite. I haven't picked out one of them yet.'

On the corner, by the ornate railed wall, a flower seller sat on a folding camp stool, bunches of flowers arranged in tissue paper in green-painted cans before her. She eyed Bodie. Thoughtfully, he pointed to a bunch of red roses and hauled out his money. Doyle watched all this. Holding the bunch of roses a little awkwardly, Bodie resumed his walk towards the hotel.

'Surprise, surprise,' said Doyle into his neck mike. 'Bought some flowers.'

Perhaps Bodie felt the strangeness of it all just as Doyle did. An elderly lady, well-preserved, walked slowly towards Bodie along the pavement. Bodie hesitated and then, moving quickly, presented the flowers to the lady. He half-bowed as he did so and then, moving even more swiftly, vanished into the entrance to the hotel. Doyle stared at the old lady and the flowers as though some secret message, or a bomb, had been passed.

The lady saw his interest in the flowers. A smile disfigured her face, for she was toothless and shouldn't have opened her mouth so wide. But she was smart.

'Red roses!' she said to Doyle, fully aware of his gaze on the flowers. 'A pound.'

Bemusedly, Doyle handed across a pound note and took the flowers. He was left standing in the street as the old woman walked off, highly gratified by this example of private enterprise. He looked at the flowers.

Almost to himself, but not so softly that his voice was not picked up and recorded, he said: 'He's in love!'

Looking across at the hotel into which Bodie had vanished at such speed, Doyle re-considered. 'Bodie? He can't be . . . No.' He shook his head. '4.5 on Alpha Charlie. Possibility cannot be ruled out that 3.7 has received fatal injury from blind archer.'

Then Ray Doyle realised the ludicrousness of the situation. Bodie had gone into the hotel, the flowers were in Doyle's hand, and people were half-looking at him in that infuriating way of people feeling superior. He said into his mike: ' . . . and man acting suspiciously. Holding bunch of flowers and talking to himself in middle of street.'

A charming girl approached along the pavements. Her skirt was just the right length, her legs superb, her head erect and her carriage wonderful. Her hair shone. Doyle dived at her, thrust the red roses into her hand, smiled his devastating smile, and hared off.

The girl did not look after him. She smiled pleasantly at the flowers. Today was the day her secret dreams came true...

Marikka splashed foamy bubbles in the bath and giggled. Bodie, who had looked into his room next door and then, at Marikka's phone call, gone to her room, smiled. Marikka lay in the bath smothered in foam, drinking champagne. Going back into the room to fill a glass for himself, Bodie said: 'Wicked...'

He went to the window to close the curtains and looked out. A man was just turning away from the hotel entrance, hovering on the pavement. That mass of curly hair looked remarkably like Doyle's unruly mop. But the man vanished beyond the railings and Bodie, flicking the curtains closed, turned around as Marikka came in.

She wore a bath towel half-covering her body which gleamed pinkly, smooth and rounded, little traces of foam flowing and vanishing on her skin. She refilled her glass. Bodie noticed there was not much left in the champagne bottle, and was glad to see a reserve waiting in the ice bucket. Marikka moved with that alluring grace he remembered, chinked her glass against his.

'Cheers, darling...' She shivered, suddenly. 'It's been a long time...'

Coming out of the hotel entrance, Max Schumann put his hand on Biermann's shoulder in a friendly gesture. He walked on so that the security men were, for the moment, left in his wake, with Kurt Kreiber pushing to keep up. Schumann took his hand from Biermann's shoulder. He looked at Kreiber, a glance of meaning both perfectly understood. It was all very neatly done. Schumann turned from Biermann to Kreiber along the pavement.

Abruptly, as though he had walked into an invisible wall, Biermann staggered. He crumpled up. Twisting, he fell to pitch face down on the pavement. The crack of the rifle shot followed almost as an afterthought.

The plainclothes security guards appeared, faces furious, already drawing concealed handguns. They clustered around the shot man and then looked up, at the hotel opposite. Two of them pointed vigorously. It was clear they had pin-pointed the window from which the assassin had fired.

The security men burst into Bodie's room. Propped against the window stood a rifle, scoped, lethal, recently fired. On the floor lay scattered cartridges and an empty cartridge case.

'Careful for prints!' The plainclothes man looked savage.

In a bunch they left Bodie's room and without ceremony burst into the adjacent room.

Bodie sat up in the chair and started to get up. His hand went into his jacket; but he'd stashed everything in the car. Marikka pulled her towel up. No one said anything. Bodie had no real idea just what was going on – there was a dreamlike quality to this – but when he saw the man standing in the doorway with a rifle held in a snow-white handkerchief, he began to wake up to reality.

He looked curiously at Marikka.

She put the back of her hand to her lips. Her face burned two brilliant spots of colour; the rest was grey with a drawn horror.

Chapter Two

The ambulance sirened up and took Biermann away. The East Germans milled excitedly, soothed by the police and the hotel staff. Unnoticed, Doyle observed.

When the security men and uniformed police came out with Bodie in handcuffs, Doyle reported in. He switched to his walkie-talkie, calling out: '4.5 to Alpha Charlie.'

Cowley's voice said: 'Alpha Charlie.'

'3.7 is being arrested. The girl is with him.'

This bombshell hit Cowley where he lived. But Doyle went on reporting: 'Looks like Willis's men – and the uniform branch.' Bodie was bundled into the police car; a woman police officer stood at Marikka's side. Doyle spoke quickly. 'They're only taking 3.7. The girl is being left behind. It doesn't look as if she is in custody.' The police-woman and Marikka began to walk back to the hotel. The car pulled away. 'Who do I follow – 3.7 or the girl?'

This was precisely the quality of predicament that made Cowley agonise over his decision. He had to think fast and he had to think right. Being the chief of any organisation, let alone one as ruthless as C.I.5, demanded energy-eroding decisions at any hour – with a firm voice, he said: 'Stay with the girl.'

Doyle's voice over the R./T. said: 'Roger.' Cowley put

his walkie-talkie away and got into his white Rover 3500. He picked up the car radio telephone on the security link and called out, and had himself put through to Willis's office.

'Willis,' he said. 'Cowley. What the hell is going on?'

'Hold on, George.' Smoothly, Willis, his slick dark hair gleaming blue in the fluorescent lighting, finished his call on the other phone. 'Firebird – vital you get prints!' Then he went back to Cowley. 'Hello, George –'

'Willis – where have your men taken Bodie?'

'I'm afraid I can't reveal that just yet. It looks pretty serious, George. There has been an assassination attempt on a foreign diplomat, and your man seems to be implicated.'

'Willis!' Cowley spoke with deep venom. 'I'm warning you. There's a dead rat under the floorboards somewhere, and the smell is coming from your department –'

Willis cut in, very coolly. 'Any firm information I receive will be passed on to you. Good-bye.' With that he rang off, firmly, smoothly, very competently leaving Cowley a prey to all manner of dark suspicions.

Detective Inspector Derek Knowles was young. That was no crime; trouble was, he looked young. He had a fresh, pink-cheeked face and baby-blue eyes and was uncomfortably aware that he did not pull as much weight as he would have liked. When the security men brought in the prisoner, Knowles had been informed. He had gathered that he had a big one in his nick.

A burly security man, all eyebrows and blue-shadowed jaws, bundled the plastic bag on to the counter. 'This is all evidence. Let's get it labelled. Careful – it's full of prints.'

Knowles took charge of the bundle and the rifle and spoke to the prisoner.

'What's your name?'

'He's a pro,' said the security officer. 'He won't talk. Only a pro would have no I.D. on him.'

Bodie knew he was on the thin end of the wedge here;

but he fancied this pink-cheeked D.I. would go by the rules.

'I'm allowed one telephone call,' said Bodie.

Before the D.I. could open his mouth, the plainclothesman said with chilling menace: 'No he isn't.'

Knowles's irritation at the heavy-handed approach of these security officers grew. 'Who said so?' He glared. 'Have you formally arrested him?'

'No,' spat Bodie. 'They haven't.'

Knowles said directly to Bodie: 'Do you wish to make a call?'

'Now wait a minute!' The security man looked upset. 'Let's take his prints first.'

Bodie flared up at this. 'You don't get my prints!'

The second security man leered at Bodie and produced his handgun from under his coat. 'They're a lot easier to take off a corpse.'

The gun shocked the pink-cheeked D.I. He looked puzzled and perturbed. 'What's the big hurry?'

'Get his prints!'

'I want to make my phone call,' said Bodie.

The moment hung and then Knowles stepped between Bodie and the gun. 'He makes his phone call, then you have his prints . . . '

The security man looked at his partner holding the gun, at Bodie, and then at the D.I. He spoke in a soft voice, startling in context, a voice that indicated he knew exactly what he was doing and had the authority to back his play. 'No. First he gives us his prints – then he makes his phone call.'

Knowles, his face fiery, spoke directly to Bodie. 'I give you my word. You'll get your phone call.'

Bodie was aware, now, that he was being railroaded. So they took his prints. So he'd let Cowley sort this lot out. He went towards the ink pad. As he did so the two security men exchanged small secret smiles, cynical smiles . . .

Using his instinctive and acquired skills at stalking, Doyle followed Marikka into the Hotel International. He checked her through to her floor and then waited, observing in a lightning-fast flash around the corner, what the set-up was. Marikka walked to the door of the suite. A man stood by the door. He acknowledged Marikka with a habitual deference and the film star went inside. Doyle carried away the immediate impression that the man outside the door was large. Very large. He filled his suit, filled it with solid bone and muscle. His head looked as though he butted down brick walls for fun. He stood there on guard. Like a brick wall himself.

Out of sight, Doyle called Cowley.

Cowley listened to what Doyle had to say and, again, took a decision. 'O.K. Listen carefully, 4.5. I want you to get her out of there. Can you do it?'

The image of that enormous guard stuck in Doyle's mind. He cupped his hands around the mike, speaking huskily so as not to be heard by that man-mountain. 'There's a heavy. Could be some fireworks.'

'You have clearance. When you get her, take her to your flat. Stand by there.'

Cowley had already given orders for C.I.5 agents to check local police stations for Bodie's whereabouts. He had also had Bodie's flat sealed off so that no one – but no one – got in there without personal permission from George Cowley.

Now he said to Doyle: 'Do you think you can handle it?'

'The guard – yes.' Doyle smiled. 'The girl – maybe!'

This, decided Ray Doyle as he stowed his walkie-talkie away and started off around the corner along the corridor, would have to be a case of the old one-two bum's rush, whoops-a-daisy. There would be no second chance. He sauntered along the corridor towards the guard at the door of the suite, casually, as though he was just a hotel guest returning to his room. He set himself, more a mental process than a purely physical. He passed the guard.

Doyle moved.

His iron-hard hand back-chopped the guard's neck in a

vicious karate blow. The guard stumbled and before he had time to realise that the ceiling had fallen in on him, the ceiling fell on him as Doyle hit him again. The C.I.5 man collected the massively unconscious body, draped it neatly, and knocked on the door. The maid, Anna, opened the door. She squealed at what she saw.

Doyle propelled the guard forward and he and Anna collapsed to the carpet in a tangle of arms and legs. Doyle leaped over them into the suite.

Marikka stood in the interconnecting doorway of the room beyond, one hand to her throat, her eyes wide. She stared, still in an emotionally-drugged state from what had happened. The telephone started ringing.

'Don't answer that!' barked Doyle.

'Who – who are you?'

For answer Doyle pointed at the phone. There was little time left. 'Who can that be?'

'I don't know – ' Marikka moved to the phone.

'Then leave it!'

Marikka jumped at his tone, and stopped going anywhere near the telephone. Anna struggled up, beginning to yell. Doyle grabbed her arm – but gently – and pushed her into the next room and locked the door. The telephone went on ringing. The guard let a groan like the wind in the Pyrenees through his flabby lips. Doyle straightened up. He pulled his jacket round neatly. He smiled.

'Would you like to see my stamp collection?'

The girl hesitated – what thoughts were running through her head fascinated Ray Doyle; but there was no time. He went to the phone, which stopped ringing. He ripped the leads out.

'It's an invitation. But I'm afraid you'll have to accept it.'

He smiled at Marikka. Ray Doyle, when he wanted to be, was just as much of a charmer as ever Bodie was. He started to organise a strategic withdrawal.

Willis ran a tight organisation, and his department brought in the results. Life was not healthy for his agents if they failed him. His red telephone rang and he gave his code name for this operation: 'Firebird.'

'I'm at the hospital.' It was Max Schumann. 'He's still alive.'

Willis frowned. This was or might be awkward. Biermann had been a Camp Commandant and should have been killed out of hand thirty years or more ago. 'Will he live?'

'I don't think so.'

'What about the bullet?'

'Your man is here,' said Schumann. 'He will get it from the surgeon.' The sound of Schumann's breathing quickened. 'And the assassin?'

'In custody. It's all working out.'

'Marikka ... ?'

'Escorted to your suite.'

The relief in Schumann's voice reached Willis, and he felt the superiority of a man who always knew where he was going. 'Good,' said Schumann. 'Now he has only to die!'

Doyle's flat was still a shambles but he found a clear space on the settee and asked Marikka to sit down. She looked pale and those twin spots of colour burned in her cheeks. She must be well aware, Doyle decided, that whatever this was all about, she could be in serious trouble. He contacted base and arranged for surveillance and asked about Bodie, to be told he had not yet been located. Then he positioned the cassette recorder to hand and pushed the mike forward. He leaned towards Marikka.

'This is 4.5 questioning Marikka Schumann. Fifteen four-seven hours.' He looked stonily at the girl. 'All right. When did you bring the gun into the hotel?'

Marikka stared back, stung. 'What gun?'

'The gun you gave Bodie. The gun used to do the killing.'

'You're crazy! Bodie didn't kill anyone. He was set up!'

'By you!'

Marikka beat her fist into her hand, agonised, wrought

up, desperate. 'We were both set up! Can't you see that!'

'I'd like to see that.' Doyle made his voice hard and ruthless, completely without sympathy. 'You prove it to me. Sweetheart!'

She sagged back on the settee. Doyle stood up, leaving the recorder running and the mike taking it all in, and started walking slowly about the room, circling the settee. She looked lovely, pale, distraught, her eyes brilliant with tears she was too tough or too proud to shed.

'How long were you and Bodie together in the room before the men entered?'

'It's hard to judge – '

'Was it more than five minutes?'

'Yes. Ten – fifteen, perhaps – '

'You're sure? You're not lying to me?'

'Why should I?'

Doyle remembered what Cowley had said – that this girl could be a spy. Her present wrought-up condition could all be clever acting. And Bodie was the fall guy. 'They were in the room within three minutes of the shot being fired. If Bodie was there as long as you say, he couldn't have done it . . .'

Some of the helplessness went out of Marikka as Doyle worked his way through. He saw exasperation on her face. 'What's the matter with you?' She spoke in a fierce, almost contemptuous way. 'Don't *you* trust Bodie?' She stood up and went over to Doyle and stared him in the eyes, seeking an answer. 'I called Bodie in the pub after I had made the room reservations through Kreiber. Bodie couldn't have been involved. He didn't have time!'

'He'd already met Kreiber before, at your instigation. They could have fixed it between them.'

'Impossible. I would have known.' She lost all that fierce attack at Doyle's insistent, wearing questions. He carried on in a strictly professional way, acting as though the man under suspicion was not his partner. Marikka put her hands to her head. 'I can't stand it! *You* are trying in your head to find Bodie guilty!'

'No I'm not! I'm trying to prove his innocence!'

'Hah! Exactly.' She took a breath. Now her colour was up. Her face showed passion and defiance and determination. 'In this country, aren't you meant to assume innocence and prove guilt?' She clenched her fists. '*I'll* stand up for him in court. I'll swear we were in that room for half an hour – even if it's against Kreiber, against my husband, against the whole goddamn East German Secret Police and the K.G.B.!'

She swallowed down, turned away, collapsed on to the settee. Doyle stared at her. An actress – a damned good actress? Yes; but Doyle had his insights, too . . .

'I'm sorry, 3.7,' he said for the recorder to take in. 'I had to be sure.'

He called Cowley on the walkie-talkie and said: 'Alpha Charlie. This is 4.5. 3.7 is clean. Repeat. Clean.'

'You're absolutely sure?'

'Absolutely.'

Cowley's sigh of relief sounded startlingly loud. 'Good work, 4.5.' Now, Cowley felt with something of the sensations of a tiger hunter with the prey in his sights, now for Willis.

Schumann came on the phone again to tell Willis that Biermann was dead. 'We have the bullet –'

'Good. Get back to the hotel.'

Willis smiled. Things were working out. The other phone rang and it was Cowley. A cautious look came over Willis's face as he said: 'Aah, George –'

'Any news?' Cowley made his tone light.

'It looks very bad.' Willis made his tone sympathetic. 'I'm afraid to say. Your man booked into a hotel room in his own name. A gun was found in the room, recently fired. The bullet has been recovered from the body and is expected to match the rifling of the gun. Prints on the rifle . . . if there are any, will almost certainly be his.' Willis admired the obvious open-and-shut case. 'I'm sorry –'

'Who was it?'

'Someone big. Afraid I can't tell you over this line.'

'Then you'd better meet me.'

'A bit pressed at the moment, old boy – ' Willis hunched his shoulder, ready to put the receiver down. Cowley's voice sharpened.

'You didn't hear me, Willis. I said you'd *better* meet me – '

'I did hear you, George. I said – '

Cowley pounced. 'You made a big mistake, Willis, setting up one of my men! Now, listen to me. We have the girl. Understand? I will use her in any way I choose in order to blow your scheme wide open.' He paused, Willis did not reply, and Cowley went on remorselessly: 'Four-thirty. The usual place. You'd better be there.'

The phone went down with a crack.

Just before he left for the meet, Willis was rung by Schumann to be told Marikka was missing. He tried to reassure the East German. He did not feel quite as confident as he had been; but his assurance and knowledge of his own power bolstered him. He drove himself, knowing Cowley would do the same, and with a great deal of antagonism concealed by their casual movements and impeccable dress, they walked slowly side by side through the park.

'George – I'm about to take the biggest single gamble of my career, and trust you.'

'You never do anything without a reason.'

'The man who was killed, Biermann, was the most militant hawk in their Secret Service. His assassination was arranged between some of his own – colleagues – and ourselves.' Willis let his gaze linger on Cowley's face, and read nothing in that lined, calm, competent face. 'The man who will replace Biermann, *if nothing goes wrong*, will be Schumann, the woman's husband. Schumann is one of *our* highest-placed agents behind the Iron Curtain. When he replaces Biermann, he will then become the highest single agent there of any Western Power.' The information stood between them, stark in its simplicity and power. 'Nothing can stand in the way of this achievement. Not even you.'

Cowley came to the point that concerned him. 'Bodie will not go to jail.'

'I didn't say he would go to jail.'

'Then what are you saying?'

'He might – escape. In exchange for the girl.'

The coldness and calculating ferocity sparked between these two like icy fire. 'And if he stays free?' There was no 'if' about that in Cowley's mind, if Willis tried to be too clever. The issues at stake were enormous; but Bodie's life was on the line, that seemed appallingly clear.

'His prints aren't on file – before this. You've always selected men with clean backgrounds. A change of identity . . . ' Willis flicked his cane about. 'He could shoot his mouth off to whoever he liked in a year or two. No one would believe him. No one who mattered, that is. He'd still be on your payroll, under a different name. All you want is Bodie. You have nothing else to gain.' Willis glanced at his watch and brisked up. 'I have very little time. And I've been straight with you. But I warn you, George, I can fight very dirty on this one, if you don't co-operate.'

Cowley had set up C.I.5 when he'd moved across from running a most successful operation with M.I.5. He understood the issues here. He thought for a moment, and it all came down to the same in the end. 'Don't double-cross me, Willis.'

With a small smile, Willis said: 'Then it's a deal.'

The security plainclothesmen infested the police station. Bodie, still handcuffed, sat in his cell and pondered the injustices of life. Once his prints had been taken he had been shut away and when Cowley called and the security men led him to the phone he felt like a prisoner freed from the Inquisition. He held the phone awkwardly, the handcuffs chafing.

'Are you all right?'

'Fine. How's Doyle?'

'Listen to me. I put Doyle on to you.'

'He's a lousy chaperone.'

'He's saved your hide. Listen very carefully. We are getting you out of there. First, put Green on the line and after he has finished, come back to me.'

The security man called Green was a cut above the others. His suit was discreetly smart and his face did not bear quite so many marks of heavy living. He took the phone and Cowley, in Willis's office, put the Security chief on.

'Green?' said Willis. 'Firebird. Let him escape.'

Green said: 'Could you repeat that, please?'

'Let him escape. He will be instructed to attempt this by his own superior, put him back on the line.'

When Cowley once more spoke to Bodie he felt that it would work out. 'They are going to let you escape. Make it realistic and proceed to a safe house.' He waited, then: 'Have you got that?'

Bodie's hackles were waving in the breeze. His suspicions were fed by well-remembered attempts at escape in the old days. 'I think so.'

'Do you want me to repeat it?'

'No.'

'All right. Report to me immediately you are clear. Good luck.'

Bodie put the phone down. He looked at the security man who smiled at him. 'All right?'

'All,' said Bodie, without expression, 'right.'

Detective Inspector Knowles looked up as the security men closed in around the prisoner, whose name he now knew was Bodie. Knowles felt impotent – frighteningly pushed aside by these heavy secret service men. His annoyance was building; but chains of command were just that – chains.

Bodie wasn't too sure he knew what the hell was going on – and whilst that was a situation that often happened until he and Doyle got it all sorted out, here and now he felt very much like the worm on the end of the hook. These security goons were too nasty for his liking. The pink-cheeked

Detective Inspector knew that, too, it was plain. Bodie again realised he knew far too much about escapes that were – helped – along by the gaolers.

The security man called Green who appeared to run the other heavies, came in and unlocked the handcuffs. Back in the cell Bodie sat down and contemplated ceramic tiled walls and scenery calculated to make a man regret a life of crime.

Green went out and checked that the other two men of his squad were in the corridor, ready. A bleeper sounded and Green took out the earplug and stuck it into his ear.

Willis's voice said: 'Firebird to Green. Revoke previous instructions. Eliminate during escape. Repeat. *Eliminate during escape!*'

Chapter Three

Make it realistic, Cowley had said . . .

Sitting in the chair in the cell, the handcuffs gone, Bodie saw the door was not only unlocked, it was partially open. He frowned. He felt like the ham in the sandwich.

In the corridor outside the security guards prowled, alert, growing more and more irritated. They kept putting their hands to the gunbutts, holstered under their armpits. Finally, one said to the other: 'He's not going to run.'

Detective Inspector Knowles looked down the corridor, his pink cheeks paler than usual. Then he turned away and went back out. He needed fresh air and walked towards the side exit of the building, the only easily accessible exit from the corridor. He stepped outside.

Bodie still sat. He listened to the soft footfalls from the corridor, feet sliding on linoleum, heard doors banging deeper inside the building. There was a dead feel to the air.

At last Green made up his mind. If the idiot wouldn't escape, to be shot whilst doing so, then he would have to be assisted to escape . . . Purposefully, two of the security men headed along the corridor for the cell where Bodie sat, waiting.

They adjusted their shoulder holsters and then pushed

the door open. They hardly got inside before a chair came flying out of the air and smashed down on the head of the first. He let out a yell and stumbled back, colliding with his comrade in rear. Bodie leaped. He drove forward. His slicked-down hair gleamed once, and then he nutted the last security man on the bridge of the nose. Blood sprayed. The guards tangled on the floor. Bodie leaped through, ran fiercely along the corridor.

He reached the end and swung around the corner as the first shots slapped out, their echoes shockingly loud in the corridor.

Running flat out, Bodie passed startled policemen and spotted the exit. He slammed through.

Knowles came alert, hearing the commotion and then seeing Bodie erupt through the exit. Bodie ran off wildly, doubled back from a blank wall, started the other way towards the parked ranks of cars and the ramp where sunlight shafted. Green appeared in the exit. His revolver snouted up. His face looked at once wrathful and blanked with purpose. He took deliberate aim as Bodie, half-crouched, sprinted for the line of cars.

Bodie was a Professional. He flung a look back. He saw Green aiming his handgun, saw that in the next second he would shoot, and he knew the security man would not miss.

Knowles stepped forward. He brought his hand down hard on Green's revolver. The gun fired and the slug skittered across the concrete. Bodie gulped and vanished beyond the line of cars.

So it had been a set-up all along the line! A 'shot whilst trying to escape' caper!

He reached the street and did not stop running until he'd crossed into a sidestreet and thoroughly thrown off pursuit in the tangle of mean streets. He was panting; but not from the exercise. The bastards!

Willis called Cowley and told him his man was out. 'Now what about the girl?'

'He hasn't called in. I'll take his word for it when he's free.'

'Damnit, George, I don't have much time to play with!'

Cowley's voice was harsh. 'No, Willis, only lives, as usual. I need this line. He may call in on it. Good-bye!'

The scheme Willis and the others had cooked up had been so sweet – and now the fall guy had escaped. Willis felt the annoyance of a good chess player whose gambit fails because of the oversight of a stupid and obstinate pawn. He sent out a general call to his department, and he sounded mean, very mean. 'This is Firebird to Special Squad. I want a man on every C.I.5 operative location we know of. Recruit from other squads from the department. You have top priority on this assignment.' He flicked the switch off and pushed back in his chair, angry, irritated. 'Cowley!' he said, viciously.

C.I.5, the Action Squad, maintained as well as safe houses various locations where equipment that might be needed in an emergency could be kept under wraps. Bodie headed for the nearest, an abandoned warehouse in a run-down neighbourhood. He broke the lock on the door and shoved it open. Inside, the place was empty apart from accumulated rubbish and dust and, in the centre, a canvas-shrouded mound. Bodie went across to a crevice between eroded bricks and retrieved a set of car keys. Then he threw back the covers, sending up clouds of black dust and setting the spiders scuttling. Under the wraps an old beat-up Cortina was revealed.

He opened the boot and took out an army issue self loading rifle. The S.L.R. fired Nato issue ammunition. With this in his left hand he opened the driving-side door and got in. Pulling down the R./T. in the sunflap he called Alpha Charlie.

Cowley answered at once, confirming Bodie's suspicions that the chief was in on this one in a big way. 'Alpha Charlie,' said Cowley. 'Proceed immediately to safe house seven!'

Bodie said: 'You have to be kidding.'

'3.7. That is an order –'

'Like the orders those cowboys had to let me escape?'

Bodie's face was drawn down, his famous eyebrows a black bar, his cheeks pinched in. He could still see that goon Green pointing the revolver at him, and feel the chill breeze up and down his spine. 'Next time I need a free passage, Alpha Charlie, I'll make my own reservation.'

Cowley spoke urgently. 'What are you talking about? 3.7. Listen to me –'

Julia who was running the R./T. rig for the chief said: 'The circuit's off. He didn't sound too happy.'

'No.' Cowley also knew about the assisted to escape routine. 'Neither am I. Get Doyle to have the girl compile a complete list, as much as she can remember, of the evidence that was removed from the hotel room after the arrest.'

If this one went wrong, Willis told himself with something of the vicious anger of a man falling out of an aeroplane without a parachute, he'd personally fry everyone who had a hand in the foul-up. Didn't that idiot Cowley understand the significance of what Willis and his department were doing? He went to a quick meet with Schumann and Kreiber in no mood to dilly-dally. The two East Germans appeared wrought-up as they got out of their car in the quiet side road and walked across. Willis got out of his car to meet them.

Schumann started off at once, almost shaking, the anxiety in him threatening to take over.

'We were guaranteed a water-tight culprit!'

'There is one.' Willis spoke easily, forcing himself to remain calm in the face of this hysteria. 'He just happens to have escaped.'

Schumann looked sick. 'What about Marikka?'

'She's not important.'

And, Willis knew, that was true, by God!

Schumann's eyes swivelled about as though he expected

half the K.G.B. to be hiding in the shrubbery. 'We have only got until Biermann's scheduled report to base this evening. Everything must be settled by then.'

'Keep calm,' Willis told him, shortly.

Saying something in German to Kreiber, Schumann swung back to Willis. He was starting to shake now. 'Don't you understand? We must have a hundred per cent watertight culprit – or we all go down! *All of us!*'

He turned quickly, almost ran to his car, followed by Kreiber. The tyres spat dust as the car took off. Willis looking after them, willed his scheme to succeed. His men *had* to find Bodie and deal with him. It was just a stupid confounded piece of pig-blind luck that the fall guy happened to be one of Cowley's – and he'd been so perfect when it began!

Doyle's new flat stood in such a position that, by an athletic climb over adjoining roofs, Bodie could squirm his way along a ledge and peer down into Doyle's window. He kept his head down and eased along to the point of best advantage. He looked in the window and saw Marikka walk past.

Absolutely shattered, Bodie sagged back on the ledge. Marikka! What the hell was she doing in Doyle's flat?

Inside his new pad Doyle paced about among the chaos without the heart even to pick up the crumpled newspapers. Marikka walked tiredly to the settee and dropped down, looking exhausted.

'If he's free,' she said, looking up at Doyle. 'Why doesn't he call in?'

Doyle fairly snapped at her. 'Would you call in? If you were in his shoes? They got his fingerprints on the rifle stock from that arcade – where you made your contact with him –'

'I didn't know how the contact was made! It was Kreiber who arranged it for me. He told me to meet him in the park.'

'All right, all right,' said Doyle and the phone rang. They both jumped, thinking it might be Bodie.

It was Cowley. 'Any news?'

'He hasn't called here yet –'

'He's unlikely to,' Cowley told Doyle. 'He saw you outside the hotel before the shooting.'

Doyle sucked air through his teeth. He could imagine. 'He won't like that.'

'I'm worried he may try something wild. We'll pick up the girl to take her to safe house seven. I've got something else for you.' Cowley was brisk, professional. 'Victor 2.8 will take over.'

The day was still warm and bright and the heat rose from the roofs as Bodie edged his way back. He felt like a target in a shooting gallery. He spotted the security man below keeping an observation on Doyle's flat. Bodie avoided him as he would have avoided a poisonous snake and reached his own car. He pondered. Who the hell was in this? All of them? What were Marikka and Doyle doing together? And that escape from the station – again he saw in his mind's eye the revolver pointing at him, and Knowles's quick reaction. Then he sat up behind the wheel of his Cortina.

From the flat came a C.I.5 agent Bodie knew – Victor 2.8 – hurrying Marikka to his car. Doyle followed, going to his own Escort. Bodie frowned. The security man, also, was taking an interest in the proceedings.

He called in to Willis on his walkie-talkie. 'Special A Seven to Firebird. Woman located! She is leaving C.I.5 flat with escort.'

Willis's voice said: 'Firebird! Special A Seven. Follow but do not apprehend. Keep calling your position.'

'Will do!'

Victor drove off with Marikka and the security goon started up and, waiting until Doyle's Escort was well out of sight, followed Victor. Bodie watched it all. He decided his best bet would be to follow Marikka and the security man. Doyle was clearly off on a job by the way he acted, and he'd be working with Cowley. That, for Bodie, was not an easy decision. He felt the world was against him, the whole kit and caboodle, and if he wanted to find anyone to trust, that one was himself – at least until he knew far more about what was going on.

Safe house seven stood, a little isolated by railway sidings and overgrown wastelands, near a gasworks. The gasholder bulked, rotund and green and black, almost completely full. The spiral ladderways crawled against the ironwork. A train passed, giving its diesel up and down note, like a mournful bird calling from the swamps. Victor tooled his car into the small drive of the house and escorted Marikka inside. The adjoining houses, all small and nondescript, like the safe house itself, gave no sign of life. The security man followed up to the road outside, letting his motor die as he reported in to Willis on the R./T. The security man did not see the Cortina that sidled into the kerb back beyond the end house. Bodie got out. He was carrying the S.L.R. and there were ammo magazines in his pocket.

Intrigued by just what was going on, Bodie climbed over the nearest wall and began his cautious approach to the safe house.

Victor, coded out as 2.8, was a large, cheerful, fair-haired man, handy with his fists. He welcomed the detail of looking after this beautiful woman; and he felt sorry that she was so clearly unhappy and on edge. Her face bore the marks of strain. Anyway, his job was to take care of her, and that, as a good C.I.5 agent, he would do.

Marikka half-turned to the door of the room. The house was furnished comfortably enough, nothing garish or obviously out of place; but the uneasiness in her persisted. As an excuse, she said, suddenly: 'I have to go to the bathroom.'

Victor nodded, half-smiling, and opened the door for her.

In the bathroom Marikka leaned against the wall and put her hands over her face. Her shoulders slumped. What was going to happen she had no idea; but she could not conceive of anything that followed the recent events as being anything happy or good . . .

She would not cry. If she believed fervently enough, she hoped, things would turn out all right. At last she lifted her face and looked out of the window over the adjoining roofs. Her face, already drawn with strain, abruptly drew into haggard lines of horror.

Bodie was creeping across the roof, a rifle in his hand, balancing with the other. And, out of his sight and waiting for him – two men, two men with guns! Two of the men who had arrested him in the hotel and who had hustled him away with so much brutal authority! He clearly did not know they were there, hadn't known they had arrived . . .

Acting with horror-inspired energy, Marikka seized up a big crockery jug from the vanitory unit. She hurled the jug at the window. The pane crashed out in a glinting smother. Marikka put her head out of the window, uncaring of jagged edges of glass, and screamed.

'Bodie! They're there! Get away!'

She pointed at the shadowed angle where the gunmen waited. Bodie looked up and saw her, saw her distraught face in the smashed window, the pointing arm. Vic appeared behind her and tried to pull her back. She struggled frenziedly.

'Bodie! Get away from here! They are all coming to kill you!'

The two security men cursed and leaped out to chase after Bodie who went slipping down the roof. He hit the guttering, scrambled along and whipped around the end. The men fired after him, the slugs hit the tiles with resounding clangs, whining in ricochet. Bodie hurled himself around the corner and leaped for the ground, jacket flying, the rifle held out to balance himself.

At the far end, between the houses, a man appeared. Instantly he whipped up his revolver and shot at Bodie.

Bodie sprayed a quick burst from the rifle that drove the gunman headlong into cover. Looking around for a way out of this mess, Bodie dived between the houses, keeping low, headed for an outhouse. The boards were grey and cracked, patched with packing-crate laths. He ducked down behind and snouted the rifle out. He could see no one.

A clatter of dislodged bricks at his back caused him to

whirl. The figure of a man dived into the shrubbery there. Bodie triggered a burst and took off, crouched over, racing for the crumbling wall. Bullets cut the ground around his feet. He went over the wall and landed in moist ferns and a pile of rusty cans. He leaped up. Directly in front loomed the monstrous shape of the gasholder. Its rotund green sides looked like the wreck of the *Titanic*, submerged in the sea for decades. The sound of running feet from beyond the wall spurred Bodie on. He raced for the gasholder.

Two men leaped over the wall. They played it clever. They did not come over together and they were spread wide apart. There was no chance that Bodie would hit both before one of them got him. He headed on, trying to find shelter in the bits of rubbish, and bullets kicked dust about his feet.

He was out in the open, swinging with the rifle, and a third man appeared and began shooting. He was trapped.

Marikka was frantic. She shook Victor, making his fair hair flop. He was a big man and he towered over her slender litheness; but she shook him like a rag doll, screaming into his downturned face.

'They're going to kill him! Why can't you help him!'

Victor dragged out his walkie-talkie with one hand and tried to hold off this shrieking girl with the other.

'Victor 2.8 to Alpha Charlie! May Day! May Day!'

Cowley's voice crackled in answer. He was living in the communications room of C.I.5 H.Q., with the immediate and expert assistance of Julia always at hand.

'3.7's showed up,' said Victor. 'He's outside – and two men – at least – are shooting at him.'

'Is 3.7 armed?'

'Yes! He's got an S.L.R.'

That sounded bad to Cowley. Bodie was the rifleman of the outfit. Willis was likely to have a lot of dead agents to bury if Bodie was feeling as Cowley intuitively guessed his own agent was feeling. The world had turned against Bodie – everyone was out to get him – that was the score, and it made Cowley savage at the way secret service bureaucrats like Willis thought they could ride roughshod over any and everything that got in their way – including a top-flight C.I.5 agent.

'They're armed with revolvers,' said Victor. 'Shall I go to assist?'

'No.' Cowley's decision was instantaneous. 'Stay with the girl. That's your assignment. There may be other gunhappy goons out there.'

Ray Doyle had been a policeman before he joined up with C.I.5 – a darned good copper, too, otherwise he'd never have made detective and never have been picked for C.I.5 in the first place. That he liked to paint pictures in his spare time had never counted against him, except in the lewd minds of his oppos who lusted after the mythical nude models he was supposed to employ. So, as he went into the station, he knew just how to pitch the approach. He mixed the friendly, all coppers together, routine, with the tough, secret, deadly ways of C.I.5 that would impress the uniform branch – if he was careful.

He went up to the desk where an old police constable stood, paunchy, a little bleary-eyed, waiting for tea break time to roll around. A young police constable, still wet behind the ears, hovered in the background. Doyle smelled the old smell of a police station, and put on his professional face.

'Forensic,' he said. 'C.I.5. That gear from the hotel. I have to check it.' He flashed his I.D. at the old constable.

'I'll have to check this.'

'I haven't got all day.'

At this the man picked up a bunch of keys and tossed them to the youngster.

'Safe room. Show him in while I check this.'

Following the young police officer, whose uniform looked too big for him, Doyle froze as the oldster called: 'Hey!'

Casually, as though nothing was the matter, and expecting the worst, Doyle turned around.

The old policeman held out a clipboard. 'You'll need this. Otherwise you'll never find it.'

The young copper took the clipboard, Doyle let his breath out, cautiously, let the old 'un have a small, almost sheepish smile at this lapse of memory, and as the youngster took the clipboard and marched off, followed him with a silent prayer of thanks to all the gods of secret agents. Reaching for the phone the veteran muttered disgustedly to himself about jumped-up whipper-snappers and their ideas of procedure.

In the safe room Doyle checked the list he had. The details on the clipboard matched fine – a plastic sack was handed across, the rifle in its plastic wrappings – and then Doyle saw the other plastic sack. Well, Marikka couldn't be expected to remember *everything*. The young police officer scratched his nose, waiting. Doyle fished around with his papers, trying to figure out how to do it. Finally, he just picked up the sack.

'That's it, then. Thanks. I'll be pushing off.'

'What's it like, in C.I.5?' The policeman swallowed, growing warm about the ears. 'I mean – is it like – ?'

'Sure,' said Doyle, going out, carrying his plunder. 'Only more than that. A lot more.'

The gunmen had Bodie boxed. Around the curve of the gasholder they suddenly leaped out, one from each side, and took pot shots at him. He ducked down. The slugs cracked past. There was no doubt they were out to kill him. He triggered a burst in reply, then swung back the other way. The other man out in the overgrown waste took a shot and the bullet bounced off the iron. There was only one way to go – and Bodie took it.

He grabbed the rough iron of the ladder railing and went up.

On the first level catwalk he had a little cover. They couldn't shoot up at him and if they showed themselves too much they might catch a burst from the S.L.R.

But they were professionals, too. They played it clever.

One angled in and shot whilst the other ran for the ladder. Bodie let rip with a spray of bullets, triggering the rifle with a vicious competence, and then started up to the next level.

Around the bulky curve of the gasholder Bodie on the second catwalk, one gunman on the catwalk below, and the others on the ground, circled around and around like squirrels around a tree. Again Bodie scrambled up the ladder, going on and up until he came out on to the convex surface. The iron rang under his footfalls. He looked over. The men were staring up. As they saw him they dived for cover.

'He's gone up!' yelled Green.

Bodie ran around the edge and then took a run up the slope, reached the top, looked down, and so circled back.

The security men began to work their way up the ladders, firing whenever they thought they saw Bodie. Bodie had two ladders protruding on to the roof to check. He had to position himself to cover both of them. He was sweating. He wasn't shaking; but the anger in his mind was beginning to make him feel that he'd have to shoot the lot of them, and damn them all. He lay on his back, the rifle ready, covering the spider-like ladder extensions. Anyone stepping off the ladder on to the roof would get a bellyful of slugs – that was for sure . . .

Clinging to the ladder just below the rim of the top, Green stuck his head over, lifted his arm and took a shot. He only just got his head down in time as a burst of rifle fire cracked past. He swore.

'He could keep us here all day! Tear gas is no good – it would blow away.'

The other security man on the opposite ladder stayed put. He wasn't going to stick his neck out. Let Firebird sort this one out.

Into the dusty open space beyond the gasholder a car screeched in to brake with a long slide. Security men leaped out followed by Willis who, instantly, took charge. One of his men produced his walkie-talkie and as others pointed to the top of the gasholder, the voice of Green sounded from the walkie-talkie.

'We've got him! He's on top!'

Another car drew up and Max Schumann and Kurt Kreiber alighted. They looked agitated and worried – scared silly.

Willis spat his orders. If this fouled-up now . . . !

In the agent's walkie-talkie, he said: 'Firebird. We'll try stun grenades.'

The grenades were brought and a security agent hurried with them to the base of the gasholder and began to climb.

The gunmen clustered at the base of the gasholder, victorious as hunters who have driven their quarry to ground. Now all they had to do was smoke him out. The stun grenades would do that. Schumann and Kreiber, talking agitatedly in German, were assured by Willis that all would still turn out well. The scheme would go through and the culprit for Biermann's assassination would be apprehended and dealt with. Then Schumann could take over his post as planned.

The grenades were delivered to Green. He hefted one in his hand.

'We want it to go off above him, right?'

'Yes. Throw it high as you can over the middle.'

Green prepared to remove the safety pin. He had a good throwing arm. He was going to enjoy this.

Up on the rounded top of the gasholder, Bodie rolled from side to side, the rifle covering each of the ladders. He was sweating now more than he liked, and he refused to think coherently of his chances. Talk about top of the world, ma – this was no way for a C.I.5 man to end up. And he still didn't know what the hell it was all about!

A smoothly streamlined Rover 3500 pulled up on squashy tyred wheels and Cowley and Doyle leaped out. Doyle looked aggressive, ready to challenge anybody. Cowley looked as though he was the cat who had eaten the cream. Tough, George Cowley; but smooth and guileful with it.

They walked across to Willis. Up on the top of the gasholder Bodie eased himself to the edge to take a quick peek at the situation. He saw. He saw the bunch of gunmen down there, he saw Willis, he saw – that was Cowley and that was his partner, Ray Doyle! What in blue blazes were they doing?

Were they in league with Willis and his mob? Was everyone against him? Was he alone against the whole wide world?

Seeing Cowley approaching, Willis pushed aside a quick and irrational feeling of unease. Irrational? Surely, yet – there was nothing the C.I.5 chief could do now. His boy was caught, trapped red-handed, and would go down for his crime – always provided Cowley would play ball.

George Cowley wasted no time. 'Call your men off, Willis. You left your back door open. You should know better than that. Doyle here collected the so-called evidence. But – he's mislaid it.' Cowley spoke firmly. 'Want to call Division?'

Security came in different coloured packages. Willis saw he had been outflanked, and the knowledge was bitter, particularly bitter as he saw the expressions on the East Germans' faces. It was their necks – and his allegiances had been with them, not the man on the top of the gasholder.

Cowley said quietly to Doyle: 'Get the girl.'

As Doyle walked towards the Rover, Willis made a wide series of gestures to his men on the gasholder, signalling them to come on down. He spoke into the walkie-talkie. 'You see me signalling. Come on down.'

Yes, security, espionage, counter-espionage – well, they were facts of life, whether you liked it or not. No amount of talking or wishing would make them go away, not in the world in which people found themselves living today. Willis would have to work out a modus vivendi with Cowley. Yes, he decided, he must do that. One agent's life was negligible in these scales. One had got away: but Biermann's assassination could not be allowed to go to waste. The East Germans would see to that, probably, and if they did what Schumann expected – then Willis shrugged. His men were coming down off the gasholder now. Cowley had won this particular round. Willis thought it would not be the last. At times it was difficult to remember they were all on the same side.

Bodie's head showed over the side of the gasholder. The rifle snouted menacingly. He looked angry, still; but puzzlement showed. Cowley stepped forward.

'Bodie! It's all over!'

The answering shout carried cynicism and awareness. 'Another escape? Like the last one?'

'We've cleared you!'

'Where's Marikka? Let me talk to her.'

Trapped though he might be on top of a gasholder and surrounded by gunmen, still Bodie was using his head. Cowley did not smile; but his little nod indicated approval. 'We have her!' he shouted up.

'Let me talk to her.'

In only a few moments Doyle returned, bringing with him Victor 2.8 – and Marikka. Her face bore the marks of strain and anticipatory terror; but she walked over the uneven ground with that lithe swing of her hips that Bodie remembered so well. She looked up, half-shading her eyes, seeking his silhouette. It was quite clear, now, what Bodie wanted from her.

'I'm all right, Bodie.'

Off to the side, Willis, still unwilling to believe it had all gone down the drain, went up to Cowley. His words were smooth, reasonable – eminently reasonable.

'I'll make a deal with you, George –'

'We had a deal.' Cowley was still looking up at Bodie. 'You reneged.'

'Bodie!' called Marikka again. 'It's all right.'

The answering yell carried chill and stark. 'You framed me.'

'No! Kreiber set me up. He and Max together. I should have known –'

'You're unbelievable!' Bodie looked down on the crowd below and this was just between Marikka and him. 'Twice in my life I trusted you and now you've made me the biggest patsy of all time.'

Marikka's shout drove up, fierce and deep and filled with anguish. 'They used me! They used us both!'

Bodie shook his head, gripping the rifle.

'Bodie! It's true. You must believe me!'

Kreiber was talking rapidly to Schumann. His face lowered with savage intent. Schumann looked ill. Finally, he nodded, turned away. His hands were gripped into fists and he stuck them deeply into his pockets, dragging down the material. He did not look at Kreiber.

The Stetchkin 9mm pistol in Kreiber's hand appeared there as though it was an old friend. No one else noticed. He moved forward.

Marikka shouted up to Bodie: 'They tricked me into it!'

Kreiber lifted the Stetchkin and fired.

At the sound of the shot Bodie whipped back off the rim off the gasholder and flattened out. The rifle clattered against the iron – once and once only – and then he had the muzzle snouted out, ready to blast the first damn-fool head to appear.

Doyle, at the sound of the shot, swung around. He had been looking up at Bodie.

Marikka Schumann crumpled. The bullet had killed her instantly, fired by an expert. She fell on to the dusty, weedy, rubbish-strewn ground. No one moved. Doyle looked at the group – at Willis, at Schumann, at Kreiber, the security men.

Doyle spoke with a welling of primitive emotion.

'You bastards!'

Waiting for something to happen, and hearing nothing, Bodie crawled to the edge of the gasholder and looked over. He saw the tableau around Marikka's body. Slowly, he took it all in. He swallowed. He still didn't understand the half of it – but he would, he would . . .

Cowley felt the disgust at Willis in him like bile.

'You got your scapegoat, after all.'

Willis nodded, and if he was nodding in agreement or

nodding at the dead girl, Cowley did not know.

'We'll have no trouble proving she was one of mine. Schumann will succeed – now.'

'Yes,' said Cowley. 'No trouble at all.'

It had happened. There was nothing they could do. Kreiber and Schumann were foreigners with immunity – and Willis's scheme would ensure they carried out the plan to the bitter end. Marikka lay on the ground, in the dirt. Cowley looked up at the gasholder as Bodie started to come down. He was old and wise in the ways of espionage. Perhaps he was better off in C.I.5, after all . . .

Bodie could say nothing. He reached the ground and threw the S.L.R. at Doyle. He walked away, over the dusty wasteground, head down, walking away from it all.

Doyle looked after him, and then said cynically to Cowley: 'Still want me to follow him . . . ?'

Who knew what was going through Bodie's mind? He had thought the world was against him, and now he had seen horror. Well, Bodie had seen plenty of horrors before and, because he was an agent in C.I.5, the Big A, he would inevitably see plenty more horrors in the future. He walked away, past the cars and Cowley stared after him. Deep furrows grooved Cowley's face. He answered Ray Doyle's question, still looking after Bodie.

'You make sure your own house is in order, 4.5.'

Chapter Four

To the cheeky pigeons who strutted across for the occasional breadcrumbs, the building site must have looked like a gigantic rubbish tip. Building materials lay scattered everywhere. Mixed in with the piles of sand and aggregate and the stacks of lumber and intestinal writhings of drainage pipes, the cement-mixers, JCBs, dump-trucks, bulldozers, all operated at maximum noise level. The noise was immense, the dust rose into the hot summer air, and – slowly, to be sure – the buildings grew.

Two concrete-mixers were chunking away, moist and grey and whirling. A man appeared from their cover, doubled up in agony, yelling. His cries were completely unheard. He was a short man, chunky, with a red and cheerful face that now was contorted in pain.

The man who followed him up, and who kicked again, hard and dirty, was bigger, tough, blue-jawed, and with a fey look in his dark eyes that should have warned the man he was now beating up . . .

From the shadow of the site office Renshaw, the site manager, looked on approvingly as Harry Bradford, the site foreman, beat the living daylights out of Joe Halloran. Halloran had proved to be a troublemaker, and manager and foreman between them knew how to deal with scum like that.

Halloran was about thirty years old, a bricklayer and good at his trade. He slipped to a knee, gasping, as Bradford smashed a foot into his guts. He retched. His insides were on fire and, despite his urgent desire to get up and put a bunch of fives into the foreman's mouth, he just couldn't seem to get off his knees.

Renshaw smiled. As the manager he could take care of himself, being a hard, dark, tough nut of a man. But his pride meant that he preferred to get other toughs, like Bradford the foreman, to do his dirty work for him. Now Renshaw moved off the steps of the site hut and swaggered across to Halloran.

He crooked a finger under Halloran's overalls and lifted him up, easily.

'All right?' said Renshaw. 'All right, son . . . ?'

Halloran gasped; but the pain was too much for him and he couldn't answer. Renshaw smiled again, enjoying his power.

'Nice,' he said, nodding approvingly. 'Not a mark. Never know our friend had a fall. Just a fortnight's bellyache.' He pushed a brown manilla envelope into Halloran's pocket. 'Got some nice medicine for that. In your pocket, son. Week's wages. And a ticket back to where you came from. And, when you get there I'd drop this habit of talking to strange coppers.'

He jerked a thumb at the painted sign over the site office.

TEMPLE-BLAKE LIMITED. Under that was: WE BUILD FOR BRITAIN.

'There's no shoddy workmanship here, understand? Understand? No handouts to council members. Things like that don't happen on any site I manage. Do they? You know that, don't you?'

Halloran slipped back into the patch of mud beyond the concrete-mixers. His face was very pale now; but unmarked, quite unmarked. All the pain seemed concentrated in his guts.

Renshaw hefted him up again, and went on speaking smoothly.

'There, he slipped and we've got all these controls. You all right, son? Now you've got your ticket. Anything else you want? Anything else we can do for you?'

At this the foreman, Bradford, lifted his mud-smeared boot again.

'No?' Renshaw spoke now with undisguised menace. 'Then get lost. And keep your mouth shut!'

Previous experience told Renshaw that his words would be heeded. No more trouble could be expected from Halloran. The site manager and foreman turned away, losing interest in the huddled figure in the mud, and walked off to the site hut for a surreptitious wet.

Groaning painfully, Halloran heaved himself up. He staggered off to the perimeter fence, where he leaned, panting, holding his stomach, in too much pain for the moment to go on any further. His body hurt – yes. But his brain was afire with entirely different feelings.

The sanctum of a senior Civil Servant ought to be tasteful, and equipped with its full quota of status trappings; in Henry Repton's case the Turkey carpet and open fireplace spoke eloquently of his exalted position. Repton was around fifty, greying a little, a vulpine academic and expert manipulator. He had done well, and the end was not in sight yet, not by a very long way.

Repton looked up as the Minister walked into the office. The Minister moved with a brisk efficiency, a politician who would, so it was said, always look around forty. His face held his habitual look of authority combined with an expression of ideological eagerness. But Repton had been undeceived on that one from the moment the Minister had arrived – the Minister was a political survivor, cunning and cautious. If there were any cans to be carried, then he would see that other people carried them.

'Repton,' the Minister said in his warm voice. 'I don't drop in often, as you know.'

'You're always very welcome, Minister.'

'If only to admire your always clean desk. Look – I'm not happy about Temple-Blake being retained on our list of nominated contractors. They could get close on to fifty million in government work this year.'

'As they did last year.'

'Last year,' the Minister said, and his warm voice carried a hint of freezing advance around the edges. 'The company wasn't facing corruption and conspiracy charges.'

'Nor are they this year, Minister.' Repton's air remained, as always, impeccable. 'Only members of their staff. And the charges are quite minor.' The way he spoke dismissed the charges out of hand.

'Oh, we know, the usual chorus.' The Minister's studied air revealed a weariness foreign to him. 'Rotten apples. But if they're in a scandal, it involves this Department, and you're not the one who has to stand up and explain to some eager back-bencher that none of the graft found its way into any pockets around here.'

'I think you'll find it'll be a purely local case, Minister. No mud. No repercussions.'

'Repton – don't be bland with me. You've been a puppet master to a dozen Ministers and you know all scandals start small. Not for me. I'm fond of my seat in the Cabinet and whatever influence I wield.'

The senior Civil Servant nodded in apparent agreement, ready to shuffle this awkwardness off in the usual way. 'I'll have a quiet word with the usual agencies, Minister. See that we're kept fully informed by the police, clerk of the court, people like that – '

'Not enough, I'm afraid.' The Minister leaned across Repton to press the intercomm button, discreet in its green-metalled and mahogany base. The Minister had made up his mind and he wanted his tracks covered. 'Mr Cowley is in reception.' Into the intercom he said: 'Would you ask him to come in, please?'

Repton's face had had long training in suavity. He betrayed nothing. But one finger tapped lightly on the embossed leather of his blotting pad, tapped lightly – and a little uneasily?

When George Cowley walked into the senior Civil Servant's room, the Minister sprawled, at ease, in the comfortable armchair and Repton himself sat at his desk, upright, suave, waiting.

Cowley sat down, making a triangle of men in the room, and came straight to the point. 'I'm not quite with you, Minister. As you know, I'm not answerable to you or this Department. Or Mr Repton here – widely known as the Cardinal Wolsey of this nation's spending in the building industry.'

The Minister touched his lips with a manicured finger. 'Not a very civil Civil Servant, are you?'

'No.' Cowley's tone was perfectly polite. 'Mostly we don't have to be. So, first, why us? Why not the Fraud Squad? Special Branch?'

'Reasons of policy, Mr Cowley.'

Cowley told him what that meant. 'The usual phrase for two coats of political whitewash.'

The Minister had chosen C.I.5 and he did not intend to be handled; he would do the handling. He took a document from an inside pocket. 'You're to keep a watching brief on the corruption case due to take place against Temple-Blake Limited. Here is my specific authority from your own Minister to involve C.I.5 in this affair.'

'I don't know what you mean by watching brief.' Cowley was fully aware of the so-far silent presence of Repton. 'If you mean I'm to see none of it gets shovelled anywhere near you or this Department, you've picked the wrong labourer.'

'Oh, no. I asked for C.I.5. I find you personally offensive and I find your Department's methods offensive. But your results are beyond question and reproach. This Department hands out a great deal of work and money to Temple-Blake –'

'And you'd like to come out of it all shiny-cheeked and

rosy and keep climbing that long political ladder.'

'Don't we all? Even you, with your tribe of licensed tear-aways. And if I were you, Cowley, I'd take a personal interest in this one. Politics is compromise and favours.'

Cowley sat for as long as he thought fit, before answering. He had a deal of work on the plate – Colonel Grigor Yashinkov had been making uncomradely noises lately – and Bodie and Doyle were out finishing up with that poor girl's torso in the swimming bath case, and, come to that, most of his agents were employed way up past their ears. But Cowley's nose, that special nose that scented the un-righteous, informed him that there was more to this inter-departmental request than he had been told.

'Compromise and favours,' he said, at last. 'And the big ears in the long corridors. The hints and the whispers and the nudges. Yes, Minister – ' He stood up and looked down on the other two. 'I'll take a very personal interest in this one because the minute my Department gets packed in any politician's do-it-yourself image kit, I get very angry indeed and I know my way around the same corridors as you do.'

With a curt but half-civil nod to Repton, Cowley picked up the file from the desk and went out. He was not pleased about this and all his professional suspicions were aroused that he was about to be subjected to political manipulation.

Watching him go, Repton allowed a tiny frown to mar his smooth professional face.

'I can see the need for political insurance, Minister. But Cowley's hardly the sort of insurance broker I'd have gone to.' His eyes surveyed the Minister with a distance set between them by their respective careers. 'Or advised you to go to, either.'

The London offices of Temple-Blake Ltd were housed in a glass and concrete ice cube. The reception area breathed money and aspirations of elegance, and the TV monitors on the walls followed exits and entrances and reported back with electronic efficiency.

In his penthouse office Tony Logan-Blake watched on the TV screen as the cameras monitored Henry Repton's approach. The penthouse was office at one end and lounging area with small bar at the other. The affluence was noticeable. Temple-Blake had built the block and chosen the best floors for themselves. Far below the foundations, the scattered scraps of iron from the lorica of a Roman legionary, his gladius and a few sesterces, lay entombed and forgotten. Temple-Blake Ltd – whose slogan was 'We build for Britain' wouldn't have cared tuppence about the legionary if they had known.

A large gin and tonic in Logan-Blake's hand matched what he considered his life style. Youngish, tall, blond, immensely confident in himself, he was one of the few whizz kids who had weathered the property trough. At his glass desk he was just finishing the day's dictation, the machine humming discreetly to itself. He thumbed the remote control switch and spoke into the machine's microphone.

'I know these opening ceremonies can be a bore, Michael, but what's the use of having dukes for friends if you can't us them to impress the top table. And I can promise you a splendid night out afterwards, and ear-plugs for the mayor's speech. Yours, Tony.' Speaking to his secretary direct on the tape, he went on: 'That's the end of that lot, darling, and we should have enough luminaries to keep all the tiny councillors happy. Whizz them around by hand, will you, with the usual "Personal" and "Confidential" blather on them.'

He switched off the TV monitor as Repton having come up in the express lift came in through the private glass doors. Logan-Blake lifted one elegant eyebrow. Languidness of conduct was a virtue taught him by Temple-Blake's Chairman, Sir James Temple, Logan-Blake's cousin.

'Evening, Henry. Without your false beard? And what brings the grey eminence of British bureaucracy into the counting house of an unprincipled capitalist like me? You know where things are. Help yourself.'

As Repton moved to the drinks cabinet, to pour a much-needed sherry from a Waterford decanter, Logan-Blake resumed his dictation. 'Oh, and, Monica, keep on to Renshaw at the Fairgate site. You know, where they're squawking about sticky fingers. I've got our legal people going to see him tomorrow and, at about fifty quid a comma, I don't want them kept waiting.'

He switched off the microphone and turned to Repton. A tiny frown marred that bland look.

'What can I do for you, Henry?'

Repton sipped his sherry and then, not so much sorrowfully as resignedly, shook his head. 'What can I do for you.' It was not a question; it was a statement.

'For a price,' said Logan-Blake. 'As usual. Your Swiss bank must be having to build extensions. Or is it Lichtenstein?'

'No, our normal arrangement is quite healthy. I thought you'd like to know you're well in line for the new health centres and I've had some enquiries from oil money. They've been put your way!'

'Then congratulations and whoopee.' Logan-Blake lifted his gin and tonic.

'Not yet.' Repton gestured with his sherry glass. 'You're in the middle of a corruption case.'

'Petty cash, new cars for councillors – isn't everybody?'

'Perhaps. But you've been getting a little obtrusive about it and I have a slippery Minister. This time he's gone beyond the Fraud Squad and Special Branch.' Repton sipped sherry, his gaze fixed on the other man. 'He's pulled in C.I.5. The others are good policemen; but C.I.5 is special. Very special. If you want Temple-Blake to stay in business – I don't care what you do – but you'd better make very very sure this current piece of bribery and corruption has a "not guilty" verdict handed down.'

Logan-Blake looked disgusted. 'A two hundred and fifty unit estate. Hell, it isn't Buckingham Palace.'

'No, Tony, but you know and I know it's the tip of a very lucrative iceberg that's been floating nicely for some years now. If anyone can sink it, C.I.5 can.' He walked across to where he'd left his briefcase and took out a folder. 'Confidential reports on some of their cases. Interesting – and formidable.'

The two men turned the pages of the file over, and, even then, perhaps, they did not recognise just what C.I.5 was – or could and would do . . .

The high-ceilinged salle rang with the slithering sounds of steel on steel. The tall windows high in the walls cast an even light upon the wood-block floor and the narrow mat. The footfalls of the fencers fell soundlessly – and then the sudden thunder of rapid footfalls broke out as one fencer essayed an attack upon the other. The styles of sabre-play here proved interesting – one man fought with consummate skill, knowing his sabre, his eye and his arm. The other fought with energy, in wide bravado, using strength and speed to prevent the more skilful swordsman's attacks from striking home.

But skill prevailed. With what appeared a simple passade one fencer drove his opponent back, his attack a brilliant series of thrusts and cuts mingled with feints that had the other man's sabre swirling empty air. The less skilful staggered back over the line.

The victor lifted his sabre in salute and then lifted his face mask. He breathed easily and was not sweating.

'That'll do for today,' said George Cowley. 'Like dancing the tango with my maiden aunt.' His tones were caustic.

The other man puffed out his cheeks as he removed his mask.

'I'm a disco man, myself, sir,' said Bodie.

Sitting with his legs crossed and lolling back, Ray Doyle smiled benignly upon them both.

'It's his army training,' quoth Doyle, airily. 'He'd rather slip a grenade in their hip pocket from behind.'

'You weren't much better,' said Cowley, tartly. 'Now,

have the two of you read the briefing on this Temple-Blake rubbish?'

Bodie nodded. 'Watching brief. Whatever that means.'

'It means,' Cowley told them, 'that you two get your best suits out of pawn, have them cleaned and pressed, and, if you don't own velvet gloves, buy some. Watch, listen and learn. Oh, and, Bodie, there are other ways of asking people questions than by removing their teeth. For one thing, it makes for clearer elocution.' He finished abruptly. 'I shall see you both up at Fairgate.'

Cowley left briskly, tucking his sabre under his arm, his helmet swinging. Quite a useful workout, if it was only against a couple of strong-arm idiots who thought you only had to hit a swordsman over the head. Bodie watched the chief of C.I.5 leave and then clumped across and flopped down next to Doyle.

'Cheers for the noble and learned art of healing.' He was still breathing just a little heavily after the bout. 'But I think the next lunch hour I get off, I'll find Cowley's new physiotherapist and tie his ankles in a neat permanent reef knot.'

'Cowley's good. Admit it,' said Doyle, stretching.

'Cowley,' said Bodie, grimly and with a wince, 'didn't climb into bed with a hangover at five this morning.'

Doyle laughed and switched up the sabre. The blade gleamed smooth and oiled, deadly in the right hands. 'Want to play?'

Bodie shook his head and then wished he hadn't.

'I couldn't take you on with chop sticks.'

The houses on the Fairgate estate had cracked ceilings, leaky roofs, junk water-piping, dangerous electrics. If a penny could be saved by inferior work, a penny had been saved. Fairgate had been put up by Temple-Blake. Sir James Temple, chairman of Temple-Blake, lived in a mansion that was palatial and well-built by honest artisans long since dead and buried. The windows of the house gleamed in their serried ranks. The herbaceous borders blazed with colour. The lawns were manicured. There were even elegant and superior peacocks, strutting about. On the sweep of the lawn a table had been laid for tea, with silver and porcelain and white napery. The sun umbrella slanted jauntily.

Logan-Blake leaned across with the tea pot. 'Fill you up?'

'No.' Robert Gillam, the firm's accountant, spoke raspingly. He had a hairline that was receding faster than the bathwater ran out through the plughole. He was impeccably dressed in formal clothes, he had ink for blood, and he was worried, dangerously worried.

Logan-Blake frowned. He looked at the tumbler in Gillam's trembling hand.

'Of course. We're on whisky.'

Gillam pushed the innuendo aside. He was watching the man on the horse who rode up gently towards the tea table. This was Sir James himself. Gillam knew about him. Sir James was third generation building money, and the knighthood had been gratefully received for generously spread, equally spread, contributions to political funds. Temple was a careful man, around fifty-eight, silvering at the temples; but he did live up to the title he had bought. His manner was languid and polished, with a little check of indrawn breath before most sentences. Logan-Blake aped him very well.

As Sir James dismounted, his hacking jacket outrageously checked, his breeches of a fine yellow-white, his boots blinding, Gillam got up and hurried forward. The incipient panic in him drove him on.

'Sir James, have you had a chance to read my memo?'

'Robert – you're the firm's accountant, so stick to that. Handle the figures, and let me worry about buying the legal brains.'

'You didn't authorise the payments at Fairgate, Sir James. I did.'

'Naturally.' Languid bonhomie shone from Temple. 'You always do as you're told.'

'Which is why,' said Gillam with the panic near to desperation, 'I'll be standing in the dock.'

'You'll have Renshaw and Bradford there with you. A site manager and a foreman.' Logan-Blake soothed in his supercilious way. 'You were deceived. You will express regret, naturally, plead pressure of work.'

'If I'm found guilty, Tony, I know enough to plead a lot more than that. There's a conspiracy charge as well and I'm not doing seven years in prison.'

A certain nervousness appeared incongruously beneath the languid charm of Logan-Blake.

'If we don't get you off, you shop us?'

Gillam suddenly realised the deep water he was treading.

'I didn't say that – '

'It's what you mean.'

Sir James smiled. He spoke in a paternal way, ironing things out, completely reasonable. 'Robert, we've been through a couple of these things before. We've paid some fines, couple of minor employees have gone to prison and we've looked after them when they've come out. Building's always been a grab bag where palms get greased. You were unlucky to have been involved in this one.'

'I've been involved in all of them.'

'Robert, Robert. One conscientious Detective Sergeant plodding away got through the outer defences.' Logan-Blake soothed with casual skill, smiling, nonchalant. 'Bad luck. That's all.'

Sir James nodded in the sunshine. 'Have a few days off.' He looked concerned for the welfare of Gillam, his parchment face expressing that concern with great skill. 'Come on, I'll get Buchan to drive you home. You're too shaky and upset to drive that big Jag of yours.'

They started to walk off across the lawn towards the gravel drive and the white-painted garages. Sir James put a concerned and paternal arm over Gillam's shoulders.

Logan-Blake looked off towards the thick stand of trees flanking the drive. Quite deliberately, giving a signal, he pointed at the back of the retreating Gillam.

In the green dappled shadows of the trees Karl Drake saw that signal. He knew exactly what it meant. Big and husky, Karl Drake, competent, held himself with a dark air of purpose; he'd been a big wheel in the higher echelons of violence and suborning for years – pay up or get smashed up was how he'd started – and now at thirty-three he had a lily-clean record. That was because of his own ability and shrewdness, and he had no intention of acquiring a record now – no way . . .

He went carefully through the woods to his Mini Clubman Estate and watched as Sir James's Rolls, uniformed chauffeur up front and the mark in the back, crunched past. It was just another job; he would do it, do it perfectly, and, this time, perhaps, take another little holiday on the Riviera. He would have earned it, that was for sure.

At the table on the lawn, when Sir James got back, a silver ice bucket with a beautiful bottle of champagne had arrived, and Logan-Blake was doing the honours. He looked up as his cousin sat down, half-smiling.

'Our Robert's turned into a bit of a nervous old woman,' Logan-Blake offered, pouring champagne.

'Always has been – started with the Gulf job.'

Logan-Blake's distant, know-it-all air complemented the silver and the champagne beautifully. 'Half a million siphoned out of that and the size frightened him. That's when he started drinking.'

'He'll crack, you know.' Sir James lifted his head and the lines under his chin tautened and stretched, like the head of a turtle poking out from his shell. 'He wants to. The full confessional.'

'I know. And he's the one to worry about. He kept count of all the private skeletons. If he goes down, we all go down, which would be a pity.' He sipped his champagne. To anyone watching them they must have seemed like two good friends, cousins enjoying a quiet drink in the declining sunlight and perhaps talking about the estates and the stables.

'I would think so. And so would friend Repton. He's

getting used to the privileges of a tax-free fortune.'

'We wove the web, cousin,' said Logan-Blake. 'And now we've got C.I.5 as the big spider in the middle. We can't play the usual rules on this one. Can we, cousin?'

They were not looking at each other. They spoke softly, in civilised tones, looking out across the lawn where the peacocks strutted, casually conversing so that their words hung in the air.

Then Sir James turned, deliberately, and looked at Logan-Blake. 'I expect you've already taken care of that.'

'Indeed. Indeed I have, cousin.'

Robert Gillam's greenhouse was L-shaped, meticulously kept up, filled to bursting within the shining glass by a profusion of brilliant flowers. Here was where a man who did not care overmuch for what he did every day could come home and relax. Flowers were Gillam's consuming passion – that, and, lately, the whisky.

Karl Drake walked down the central aisle of the main arm of the L-shape and touched some of the flowers, not feeling their warm soft silkiness through his gloves. Above the neat potting bench with the white porcelain sink and taps next to it hung a large wooden cupboard, painted green. Drake unlocked this, with the key he'd been given along with his instructions, knowing just how much time he had before the owner of the greenhouse stepped out into his garden.

The shelves contained packets and bottles of weed killer, locked away here for safety, prominently marked 'Poisonous' and 'Keep out of reach'. From a small separate compartment in the side of the cupboard Drake reached down a bottle of Bell's. The glass at its side was clean.

Drake checked the level of whisky in the bottle and then from his bag produced another bottle of Bell's. He poured away the amber liquid down the sink until the two levels were identical. He placed his bottle in the cupboard, and Gillam's bottle in his bag. Then, he reached up and turned over the golden cardboard bell hung on its yellow string around the neck, changing BELL'S to OTHER FAMOUS BELLS. He nodded, satisfied.

Then, quite calmly, he walked around the L-shape into the shorter arm and sat down on the brick edging, where pots draped bunches of flowers and the sun shone in, low and level and comforting. For this kind of money, on a job like this, he could wait a long time, wait patiently, wait like a hunter out for the kill.

He did not have long to wait. Gillam's worries brought him out to the greenhouse for more than a mere walk among his beloved flowers. The accountant's face creased with the near-panic that threatened to engulf him. He placed his briefcase down among the pots and unlocked the cupboard and took out the bottle of whisky. He held the glass up to the light, and although it was perfectly clean, gave it a fussy wipe with his spotless handkerchief. Then he poured a generous slug.

His nerves were shredded. He took a big gulp of whisky. He made a small grimace at a taste he could not quite identify with the smoothness of Bell's. He shook his head, took another drink.

He sat on the brick edging for a space – and then he doubled up as though kicked in the midriff. An expression of awful pain flooded over his face. His insides were afire. He tried to shout and only a ghastly whooshing shuddered from his contorted mouth.

He crashed over sideways and smashed the bottle on to the brick as he fell, smashing it into glinting shards. He collapsed on to the wooden slats, twitching, shaking, his feet drumming.

Karl Drake sat quite still for a space longer.

Then he got up and walked carefully around the L. Gillam lay sprawled out in death. One hand still crushed a flower head where he had made a last spasmodic clutch at life.

Drake stood over the body.

'Dear, dear,' he said, but so softly the words barely brushed the air, inaudible. 'You would have to break the bottle, wouldn't you? Make everything messy.'

Moving with a steady confidence, he took the original bottle of Bell's from his bag and replaced it in the cupboard. He reached down a bottle of weedkiller, poured some down the sink, splashed more around the glass that had broken in Gillam's hand.

Painstakingly, he picked up all the pieces of broken bottle. He put them carefully into his workman's bag. He looked about. The place looked clean. But he was a pro. He went over it again and he smiled with pleasure at his own thoroughness as he found a small splinter tucked away in a crack of the wood. That went into the bag, too. Then, still quietly, still calmly, he went out of the greenhouse. Robert Gillam lay on the floor. His worries about Temple-Blake, about drinking, were over. So was his love of flowers.

The building site looked just the same as any other, or almost any other. The wire-mesh perimeter fence had no breaks in it that would admit petty thieves. An Alsatian guard dog, on the inside, squatted back on his hind legs and lifted his fierce head and barked furiously.

Up on top of the fencing Doyle stopped what he was doing. What he was doing was climbing the fence to drop down on the other side. On the guard dog's side. That did not seem a good idea right now.

'Geddown,' said Doyle, hanging up there like a fuzzy-haired angel on a wire. 'Geddown, boy . . . All right . . . I only want to look. All right?' The dog went on barking ferociously. 'Please,' pleaded Doyle, hanging on the wire. 'Little monster.'

Bodie walked up from the parked Capri, smiling in his infuriating Bodie way.

'Shurrup!' said Bodie.

The dog did so.

'You,' said Bodie, smugly. 'Don't know how to talk to a dog.'

Thankfully, Doyle dropped down from the fencing. He dropped down outside, away from those gleaming fangs.

'I've seen you talk to a few dogs in your time.'

'Don't you want to have a look?' Bodie quizzed down his famous eyebrows. 'It's a watching brief. Ergo – we ought to watch.'

'There's nothing to see.' Doyle made himself a liar by his baleful look at the Alsatian, who was panting now with a passion that, Doyle knew, was reserved for him and him alone.

Bodie looked through the fence. 'Just a place where there's a lot of hard graft.' He thought about that. 'Graft . . . '

'Maybe we'd better come back when they're open for business. There's a man who wants to buy us a drink waiting.'

They drove around the shabby streets until they reached the Crown and Anchor, a public house with shiny tiles and fresh brick, with old brasses and plastic furniture. It quite clearly didn't know what sort of establishment it was. They went in and leaned up against the bar, surveying their surroundings with some distaste.

'Hardly your class of cocktail bar, old man,' observed Doyle.

'I always like a place where you can spit on the floor.'

'After,' said Doyle, quick with it. 'You've asked for the sawdust, mind.'

'Are you sure this is where he said to meet us?'

'Specific,' said Doyle. 'Down to the betting shop opposite and the knock three times and ask for Fifi next door.'

'What does he look like?'

'Don't you know?'

Bodie didn't answer. He looked about the pub. The place was slowly filling, and it was clear a lot of the local brickies and labourers came in here for their ritual wet after work. A short man, chunky, with a mop of hair not unlike Doyle's curly cap, stood by the bar quietly supping. His clothes were rough workman's clothes, but clean and unsoiled by a day's toil. The doors opened and two men came in, talking in loud confident voices. When they saw the chunky man with the red face at the bar, their voices took a sharper edge.

The tough with the blue-jaw said: 'Look who's down there, Mr Renshaw.'

Renshaw, the site manager, looked. A dark, hard nut of a man, he was supremely confident in his own surroundings – like on a building site or in a pub . . .

'Your pal with the bellyache, Bradford.' Renshaw spoke with a bite. 'He was supposed to have left by now.'

'Perhaps he's waiting for his nice policeman friend so he can spread some more dirt about the building business.'

Listening to this – unable not to hear it all – Bodie and Doyle exchanged glances. They eased upright at the bar.

Bradford ambled towards the chunky man.

'You're supposed to have gone home, son. What about it, then, master brickie? Come in for some gripe water, have you?'

Doyle was nearest. Bodie tapped his partner on the arm. Bradford swung his fist back all ready for the first deadly, fight-winning blow. Doyle moved with deceptive speed, caught Bradford's arm as it swung back for the blow. Doyle spun the foreman around like a yo-yo, tripped him, sent him staggering across two chairs and a table. The noise started to build up.

Renshaw saw this unprovoked attack upon his foreman and, without wasting words, drove in hard to get this tousle-haired freak. He was suddenly met by a smooth smiling man, a man with sleek dark hair and eyebrows that expressed perpetual delight and surprise at the world's quiddities. Renshaw lashed out, and the man was not there, and something very hard and very painful drove in between the site manager's ribs.

Both Renshaw and Bradford were experienced pub fighters. They could handle themselves. They were effective, dirty and confident. They'd put these two slickers down, kick them a few times, and then get on with the real business.

It didn't work out like that.

For one thing, when they tried a good old reliable dirty trick, it was met by a trick of even dirtier hue. For another, and they began to realise this as the fists flew, the boots kicked and the heads butted, these two weirdos were just too quick, too strong and too good for the builders. Renshaw and Bradford fought hard. Bodie and Doyle handled them. Tables and chairs went over, a few glasses smashed to smithereens. Other patrons of the Crown and Anchor hurriedly snatched up their drinks and scuttled off out of the way.

Renshaw's face hit the floor and skidded.

Bradford went over sideways and landed to gaze blankly at the underside of a table. A drop of spilled Mackesons dropped on to his face. He didn't care. He didn't know.

The two C.I.5 men straightened up, smoothed their clothes. Bodie put a hand across his hair – it was a waste of time for Doyle to do anything so foolish – and then rubbed his hand.

'I,' said Bodie, solemnly. 'Enjoyed that.'

Doyle went over to the chunky man whose hair had been cut from the same mop as Doyle's. 'You Halloran?' He held out his hand. 'I'm Doyle.'

They shook, and Bodie said: 'Bodie. You chose a funny way to introduce yourself.'

'Yeah.' Halloran looked at the recumbent pair, and then back to the partners. 'Just wanted to make sure whose side you're on. Too many of you fellers are bent. Get you another drink?'

Doyle digested this little sermon in silence.

Bodie smiled and picked up a broken glass.

'Think I could have a clean glass?'

Chapter Five

The vegetable oil in the stainless steel pans bubbled and the chips came out in the scoop golden brown and delicious. The fish held that golden promise of white flaky flesh, and the white paper was not newspaper. Halloran, Doyle and Bodie sprinkled salt and vinegar lavishly and Bodie popped a chip into his mouth before they'd left the fish and chip shop. The queue shuffled up three places.

Outside, the street looked normal. Doyle gave the place a swift look as they walked along, dipping into the papers spread on their left hands.

Halloran chewed and then said: 'I can't believe it, can I? All I was trying to do was my good citizen act. You know, see a bit of graft, say this won't do, so I go down to the local copper shop. That estate's a disgrace. Then I find I'm really in it.'

'How?' said Bodie around a chip.

'How d'you mean, how?'

The aroma of fish and chips and vinegar wafted with the three as they walked along. 'He means,' said Doyle, 'he doesn't understand these things. More used to going around with his face blacked –'

'And a knife between my teeth. Like you – quite the little crusader. Go on . . .'

'If that's what you want.' Halloran picked a fish bone from between his teeth. 'I go to see the big boy, local big chief. He says there's not much in it. Not worth bothering about. Just rumour.' He popped a chip, chewed. 'Then someone higher up must have got wind of it, someone they must've left out. He wasn't getting his share, so he gets up tight about being left out, I suppose.'

'And those two?'

'You just done over?' Halloran smiled, swallowing down, thinking of the beautiful slumbering scenery they had left in the Crown and Anchor. 'He was right. Small fry. Rubbish. In for a few bob, skimping on materials, being light on the concrete mix. So that makes them a few thousand quid. But we're talking about millions.' They parted to let a housewife and her shopping basket through. 'Millions – going to the top – spread over years.'

Doyle said: 'And Councillor Webb?'

'Another one. Chairman of the local housing committee. Charged along with them two. Caught with his hand in the till. Bet that surprised him.' Halloran did not snigger; but he might well have done. He had cause. 'But they won't prove nothing. Because they're all tiddlers like me, caught in the big pool.' The humour left Halloran's bruised face. 'Bit of scratch my back under the old pals act – and they're free ...'

'Doesn't change much,' observed Doyle.

Halloran looked across. 'Ex-copper?'

Bodie smiled. 'You can always tell. Experts on graft.'

'Thank you.' Doyle's tone froze. 'You'll have to excuse his manners. He doesn't have any. But I still don't see – '

'How it all happened? All them nobs at the top. I suppose someone put the bite on. Asked to see the books. They went for Gillam, the Temple-Blake accountant. Must've thought, here we go, here's a brick we can prise loose.'

'Gillam?' said Doyle. 'You reckon he's someone we ought to see?'

'Yeh.' Halloran wiped his lips. He crumpled the empty paper and tossed it into a disposal bin fixed to a lamp-post.

'Yeh, you ought. Buy yourself a harp and a couple of wings. Don't you read? They found him last night with his toes turned up.'

For George Cowley a watching brief meant finding out about the things and people he was supposed to watch. The hotel the local big wigs used stood on its own site as though the town had grown up around it. In non-physical terms, that is; in respect of the men who frequented the bar and lounge, that was more than half true. The plush had faded on the curtains and they hung heavy with the dust of decades. The furniture and fittings were durable mahogany and the ornate plasterwork of cornice and ceiling was browned past yellow from the nicotine fumes floating from pipes that had changed from Bulldogs to Dunhills and now were giving way more and more to film-wrapped packs of panatellas. Green baize aprons were in evidence in the remoter regions. The waitresses wore white caps and aprons over their decent black dresses; and they boasted as they gathered in the service corners of their great-grandchildren. The manager drank madeira.

Such places form the skeleton of the country's infrastructure, and thrive on respectability and tradition. The queen they would like to refer to would be Victoria. Cowley sat at the bar cautiously sampling a malt whisky. In the adjoining lounge the armchairs could house a herd of elephants without yielding a fraction of an inch. In there, local councillors discussed ratepayers' money and the best way of spending it to show well, and of screwing more. Most of them were honest, well-intentioned. But in this particular barrel there was more than one rotten apple.

Councillor George Webb sat at the bar along from Cowley and finished up his drink. He called for another. That would not be his second of the day. Webb was a rotund fifty or so, bathed in the self-importance of small authority, a joiner of societies, blazered, club-tied, a party wheel-horse who mistook his support by an apathetic electorate for recognition of his non-existent talents.

Now he called to two other men, somewhat removed past the glass display. They were like him in many ways. They were all part of the scenery here.

'Not very sociable, tonight, are you, Harry?' called Webb. 'How about one with me?'

'Not tonight, George.'

Webb sniffed. He had a round red face with a large, black, downdrooping moustache. He thought it gave him an air of distinction. 'Least you could do, as my Deputy Chairman.'

'Acting Chairman, now.'

The two men finished their drinks, somewhat hastily, and moved away. They did not look back.

Webb downed his own drink and put the glass back on the bar with some force. He swung in his chair and glared down at Cowley.

'Never credit it, would you? Bit of trouble and nobody wants to know you. I used to be able to come in here any time and it'd be: "Hello, George," and "What are you having?" Half the council in here.'

'They were abrupt, I'll say that.' Cowley lifted his glass. 'Why don't you have one with me?'

The barman took the glasses and creaked off to the optics. Webb's features showed a little brightening around the edges. He came down the bar and he and Cowley shook hands.

'Always the same.' Webb shook his head. 'Takes a stranger to show some civility when your friends turn their backs. I'm George Webb. And I'm still Chairman of the Housing Committee, never mind what crawling Harry Braithwaite says.'

'Responsible job.'

'It is. The biggest.' Webb took the fresh drink, swilling as he recited the things that mattered in life to him. 'Ensuring decent dwelling-units for the citizens of this community. It's big George Webb they've always had to rely on. Big George Webb'll see you right! Years I've put into it.' Now he was growing morose again. 'They've always known they could come to me.'

Cowley signalled the barman again.

With sympathetic nods and murmurs of understanding, Cowley listened as Webb expounded on the ingratitude of humanity. They adjourned to the dining-room, a vasty cavern of browns and greens in which the starched white table cloths floated like lilies on a shadowed pool. An elderly waiter hovered tactfully and did not risk a second hernia by pulling the heavy mahogany chairs out for the diners. They went on talking as they ate, a thumping meal, solid and only partially digestible.

'Responsibility. That's what the new fellers don't understand. The personal touch. Get to know your contractor.'

'Is that,' said Cowley, 'the trouble you mentioned?'

'And look where it got me!' Webb attacked his beef with massive cutlery and massive gestures. 'Chairman of Housing, been on the Council for twenty years and there was this estate and they reckoned there was a bit of fixing, corruption, whatever they call it.'

'I've yet to know public service get the appreciation it deserves.' That, thought Cowley, was damn-well true.

'I remember when they lived in whippet kennels.' Webb forked the overdone cauliflower. 'We had trams on the High Street. Lucky if you had the price of a ticket to get on. Think they're grateful? I spend most of my free time at it and I know. Pennies for expenses and precious little thanks.'

The meal wended on in much the same vein, and Cowley listened and stored the information away. Later they moved to the lounge and the elephantine armchairs. Webb sank down with a grunt as the waiter shuffled forward.

'Don't mind about it being after closing-time. They're used to me here. I was telling you about Jim Renshaw. Good site manager. Appreciated me taking an interest in the job. If he's got a pal in the travel business who can get me and the missus a couple of weeks in the sun and I'm paying, mind, cut price and I'm paying, and if he's got enough consideration for his work force to have them do a few bits of things around my house when they're idle, instead of laying them off, well – ' He accepted the drink and lifted it, staring at Cowley. 'Well, I can't see what's wrong with that.'

'Nasty minds everywhere.'

'Nasty enough to get me took to court. Some building inspector running snivelling to some interfering detective-sergeant just because I wouldn't uphold his complaints about the state of Renshaw's job.'

'You meet a lot of them,' said George Cowley, chief of C.I.5. 'If only people would mind their own business.' And, on that, Cowley drank up.

On the following day Logan-Blake received his expected visitor. The penthouse suite glimmered with sophistication and obtrusive affluence. It was modern, sleek, efficient. George Webb, ushered in by Logan-Blake's secretary, appeared an anachronism in these surroundings, like a grubby character from a Victorian novel studied for Eng Lit. But he was prepared to bluster along as he always did, and, now, as he must if he was to do the right thing.

'Come in, Mr Webb, come in.' Logan-Blake's manner would have charmed a dowager duchess – had done so. 'Can I offer you something?'

'No, thank you very much. I've had to take the whole day off as it is. And you know what business is like these days – '

'Oh, I'm sure we could compensate you for that.'

'I'm not worried about that. And I don't mind helping.'

'I should think you don't. You'll be in the dock.'

Webb's black moustache shivered as he blew out. 'And I hope you'll be out front, listening. If not you, one of your colleagues.' He put a hand inside his blazer. 'The clerk of the court's an old friend – and he knows it. That's the only reason I got the list of jury members.' Webb took out the paper with the list of names.

'What are friends for, if not to help each other?'

Logan-Blake took the list. He tapped it. 'Twelve good men and true.'

'With,' said Webb with a great deal of his fat bonhomie returning. 'Names, occupations and addresses.'

'I think,' observed Logan-Blake with a suavity that should have chilled any man with sensibility. 'I think you'll be able to sleep at night now, Mr Webb.'

After Webb had gone, red of face and resuming his self-held opinion as a pillar of the community serving his fellow citizens, Logan-Blake welcomed his cousin, Sir James Temple.

'It is good news, cousin, on the Coroner's verdict. Robert will be laid to rest. *Felo de se.* While the balance of his mind was disturbed.'

Logan-Blake said: 'Henry Repton called.'

'Whispering, naturally.'

Logan-Blake looked across. 'Reminding me that the full verdict of "Not Guilty" is still essential and that a man called Cowley might be round with some awkward questions.'

'Your ball,' said Sir James, half-lifting a hand, languidly. 'You've always been good at answering those, cousin.'

The really disturbing thing in this whole messy business, it seemed to Cowley, was the continuing canker of selfishness, of self-interest carried past the bounds of normalcy. He and Bodie and Doyle were not dealing with the false-glitter of apparent surfaces of society, the advertisements, the romantic conceptions, the drug-addictions of hectic living, the colour supplement life-styles. Ordinary people were living in houses that were little better than death-traps. Pest-holes. And greedy men had pocketed money to shuffle off this shabby chicanery. It was going on all the time, always had, old boy, always would. But modern life demanded something a little better than pure self-interest. The country was going to the dogs, everyone said so. These fat sharks were helping the ruination by their corrupt practices. C.I.5 had been called in to watch. Cowley took

Bodie along with him to see Colonel Nigel Summerville, and he was growing more and more convinced that, political pressure or not, the watching brief gambit was almost over.

The Gentleman's Club was overlooked by Old Nosey on his tall column where he could have a chat every now and then with Nelson on his. The entrance was columned and porticoed, and the interior was mahogany and silence. Colonel Summerville greeted Cowley where they could talk, and as they shook hands eyed Bodie.

'I say, Cowley, did you sign *him* in?'

'Yes, Colonel. He works for me. If you use the term loosely.'

'I remember the days when this used to be a military club.'

Summerville's white hair gleamed in the light from the cut-glass chandelier. His nose was bulbous, decidedly so, and his eyes held a fishy expression that belied his acumen. He wore a Royal Engineers tie.

'He was military,' said Cowley. 'Once.'

'Oh.' Summerville waved them to the massive armchairs. 'One of those rag and bone regiments creeping about behind enemy lines. Looks the type.'

Bodie was amused by this. The old boy had an eye. 'I could never find a bowler hat to fit me,' he said, dead-pan.

Cowley knew just what he wanted. 'Colonel, I want to pick your brains. First, this Temple-Blake case.'

'Oh, that'll blow over. Storm in a concrete mixer. They're always buying these fat little councillors and giving motor cars to sub-contractors. If a contract's worth a million or two it's worth greasing a few palms.'

'What about Temple-Blake itself?'

Summerville blew a resounding breath. 'They've only done a couple of contracts for us at the Ministry of Defence. Both shoddy. Won't have them on parade any more. Hasn't stopped them doing well, though. Chap called Logan-Blake. He's the sharpy. Sir James, who's supposed to be the boss, just swans around, pouring out the charm and free champagne.'

'Would you say they were crooked?'

'Oh, yes, of course.' Summerville spoke quite naturally. 'In a big way. When people have a lot of work to offer they expect something in return.'

Bodie, smoothly, said: 'What do people offer you, Colonel?'

'Courtesy and civility, young man.' The Colonel shot it back, sharpish. 'And that's all. They'd get the back of my hand if they offered a farthing.' He turned away from Bodie's uncouth youth and said to Cowley: 'My advice to you is, get hold of the figures and a good cost accountant. I think you'll find the skimmed milk went into the contract and the cream into Logan-Blake's pocket.'

'You,' Cowley said. 'Can be a slanderous old devil when you want, can't you?'

'You've never had a very high reputation for tact yourself, Major. I can remember the names you called me just because I was trying to dynamite a bridge. And you needed it as a convenient trap to shoot people.'

'Every man to his trade.'

Summerville raised his eyebrows. He spoke with a nostalgic note in his fruity voice. 'That's when we had a trade, old boy. Not marching desks or detonating filing cabinets. If you're after this Temple-Blake lot find the books, get the figures they publish and the figures they don't. That's where it'll be. And good luck to you.' He levered himself up out of the chair like a pot-holer escaping from a cave-in. 'I must go now. There's game pie on.'

As the Colonel marched out, straight backed, his white hair gleaming, Bodie looked after him and then across at Cowley.

'Is he real?'

'Realer than most.' Cowley was tart. 'And so's his advice.'

Karl Drake was a very useful man to have around working for you. He was meticulous, tireless, super efficient and deadly. Logan-Blake had no fear of meeting with Drake in the penthouse suite of Temple-Blake. Drake was clean. He handed across the list of jurors George Webb had given him.

'There's the jury,' said Logan-Blake. 'And I want them all to sing in harmony.'

'To the tune of Not Guilty.' Drake nodded. 'Any particular method?'

'Up to you.' Logan-Blake knew when to delegate. Robert Gillam had been an object lesson. 'Everybody has a pressure point. Greed, envy, resentment, fear. Don't tap all of them. Find two or three of the easily persuaded ones and make the incentives high enough.'

Karl Drake smiled, a wolfish smile that had appeared when many people had suffered grief in the past. 'Or low enough.'

Logan-Blake smiled in return. 'Yes . . . '

The weeding-out of unsuitables took Drake little time and he made his first call on William Musgrave at the hardware shop where Musgrave was deputy manager. He looked tired and on his face the lines of soured ambition told Drake this one would be touchable. A simple appeal to Musgrave's sense of grievance, that the men in the dock were being fixed, and a down payment of five hundred now and five hundred after the verdict, convinced Musgrave.

Aubrey Singleton was handled differently. Singleton was an ineffective teacher of sociology, a complete waste of time in Drake's book, and the threat of exposing him to a fake charge, of – for instance – setting his wife up for a shop-lifting charge that would stick, and of – frightfully – threatening to have his children run over outside the school, reduced Singleton to a shattered wreck. He promised – and no money changed hands.

Drake left off gripping Singleton's arm with a grip that shocked by its savagery as much as by its strength.

'You do it,' said Drake. 'Not Guilty. And, you never know, there might be a few quid through your door one night and you could buy a new suit.'

Drake nodded affably, leaving Singleton quivering, and sauntered out of the Adult Education Centre, very smooth, very assured, lethal as death itself.

Without relishing the interview, Cowley went to see Logan-Blake. He took in the sumptuous surroundings, the chrome and glass, the stainless steel, the super-efficient secretaries, the electronic equipment. Logan-Blake was distantly polite, offering glossy brochures of the firm's successes, talking about vanishing profit-levels. The visit was another aspect of the watching brief. When he left, going down in the Express Lift and out beneath the colossus of glass and concrete, Cowley realised he was sick to the back teeth with the watching brief.

The verdict on the corruption case was coming in and he went along to the Crown Court. Bodie and Doyle were there – part of their watching brief – and the sense of dissatisfaction gnawed at Cowley.

When the jury filed back into court, the judge, for one, anticipated no problems. The foreman of the jury was Aubrey Singleton, the natural choice, a teacher of sociology with the slightly out-of-elbows liberal gentility of the theorist. He looked pale and nervous.

'Ladies and gentlemen of the jury.' The judge's voice rolled in the time-honoured words. 'Have you reached your verdict?'

Singleton stood up. He swallowed. 'We have, your honour.'

'And what is that verdict?'

'Not guilty, your honour.'

The stir buzzed around the court like a breeze through a wheatfield. The judge's summing-up had perfectly clearly indicated that a guilty verdict was the proper one. In the double row of jurors, Sam Burton scowled. He lived on the damned Fairgrove Estate, and his house was a mess. He and the neighbours took in each other's work – Alf from over the road doing the electrical work, Sam doing the plumbing. But it was a constant struggle against rotten workmanship and rotten materials. If these bastards had been found guilty perhaps something might have been done.

Musgrave, pale and sweating, pushed a finger across his upper lip, and then wiped the sweat off his finger, shaking.

Among the policemen, George Webb smiled with relief. Of course, with his friends, there'd been no need to worry, had there? As for the site manager and foreman, Renshaw and Bradford, they were openly laughing, one at the other, feeling the sudden gush of relief.

The judge breathed heavily.

'And is that the verdict of you all?'

Singleton said, his voice a squeak: 'The verdict of a majority of us, your honour.'

The judge nodded to indicate Singleton might sit down. He stared at the jury. He felt the dissatisfaction, and he spoke with heavy emphasis.

'First, ladies and gentlemen, may I thank you for the obvious time you have taken over your deliberations which I consider only commensurate with a case of corruption which involves taxpayers' money.' He moved his head from side to side, staring at the jury.

'I must confess a little surprise at the verdict of Not Guilty, albeit on a majority decision, and could wish that you had paid less attention to learned counsel's emphasis on the wholly hypothetical ring-leader activities of the defendant who committed suicide. I must, however, bow to your decision and let the verdict be so entered. The defendants may step down.'

So, that was that. The court emptied in due procedure, and Cowley looked balefully at his two star agents in the corridor outside as the busy activity of the Courts bustled about them.

Bodie sniffed. He pointed at Doyle.

'Smells worse than his socks.' His face expressed the dedicated desire of a C.I.5 agent to get out there in the field. 'When are we going to get back to some real work, sir?'

Cowley humphed. 'When I say, Bodie.'

Doyle and Bodie exchanged looks. The chief was not a happy man – and that boded ill for some hapless wight.

Bodie was absolutely right – on two counts. There was a smell and they ought to get down to some real work. George Cowley knew Bodie was right. When he received the call from the Minister, he had a shrewd idea of just what the coming interview had been called for – and a suspicion that it would not go the way the Minister expected.

Henry Repton's senior Civil Servant's sanctum looked just the same. It breathed of the heart-blood of the corridors of power. The Minister and Repton stood by the tall window as Cowley came in, and they turned to face him together.

Cowley said: 'You sent for me, Minister.'

The Minister did not frown; but a look he instantly quashed crossed his face, a tiny look of irritation.

'Asked if you could spare a moment. There's a difference.'

Cowley made no reply, and the Minister went on, putting that old familiar warmth into his politician's voice.

'Purely to say thank you for your efforts on behalf of this Department over the Temple-Blake corruption. And I think the Not Guilty verdict clinches it, don't you?'

'No.'

The Minister breezed on. 'Of course it does. Entirely satisfactory. No scandal, no fuss, no repercussions – '

'And not a single scratch on your shiny armour, Minister.'

The Minister sailed through these remarks of Cowley's like a battleship sailing through a congregation of dories.

'Then thank you for your help and I'd be glad if you'd convey my appreciation to your colleagues.'

Cowley stared at the two men for a moment – at the Minister with his pompous and yet calculating way, and the Civil Servant with his secretive smooth manner. If it had to be said, Cowley would be the one to say it – that was why he was chief of C.I.5.

'When I am assigned a case at C.I.5, it gets closed only under my personal signature. I didn't want this assignment. I regarded it as a trivial matter of image protection.' He spoke still with that same plummy voice; but the words were cold and jagged. 'Since then a man has died.'

Repton made a dismissive gesture. 'The verdict was suicide.'

Cowley went on in that harsh relentless way. 'And, in my opinion, a jury has been suborned. It now takes on all the aspects of a case in which my Department cannot relinquish interest.'

The Minister let Repton make the running. The Civil Servant spoke icily. 'You can be forced to do so, Cowley.'

There was no need for George Cowley to shake his head. His eyes were perfectly steady, his mobile mouth forming his words and his plummy voice stating them with a finality that, suddenly, made the pomp and circumstance of the Minister and his Civil Servant the hollowness it was.

'Not by you, Mr Repton, nor by you, Minister. I'm allowed a certain degree of latitude and I have already put on record my distaste that the Department I run should be used for Ministerial public relations protection rather than its proper work.' The chill of reality, of the real work and the real world, enveloped the two men listening to Cowley. 'We can now begin that work.'

Chapter Six

There hung about the building site a new atmosphere – oh, the dust and the smells still clung; but Renshaw and Bradford were off the hook, scot free and laughing. Halloran took Cowley along to see the site. The site hut still stood where it had been when Halloran took his going over from the manager and his foreman. Now, Halloran believed, maybe the boot was on the other foot – bovver boots with metal caps.

Doyle parked his white Escort away along the fence and walked quickly to catch up with Bodie, who was watching Cowley and Halloran. Bodie jerked his thumb.

'What are we doing here?'

'Good question. This is where it all began. You know the master. He needs something to tickle his itch.'

'So tickle his itch.'

Doyle looked at the piles of lumber and the dump trucks and made a face. 'Want to build a house or two while we wait?'

'Not,' Bodie told his partner, 'in these shoes, thank you. Anyway, you touch any of this stuff and your pal Fido will greet you – with his teeth.'

'Him,' said Doyle. 'I'll sick you on to him – birds of a feather, you know.'

Renshaw kept his gaze fixed on Halloran. Then he came out of his site hut and advanced menacingly. 'Hello, runt. Thought we'd seen the last of you.'

'Did you, Mr Renshaw?' Cowley spoke with soft ease.

'Who are you?' At Renshaw's belligerent tone, Cowley took out his I.D. and showed it. 'Oh,' said Renshaw. 'Official call?'

'Not really.'

'Then this is not a public park. This is a private building site. All visitors got to have passes. State their business.'

'Or they get beaten up, Mr Renshaw?'

A dump truck clattered and clanged past, spitting globs of dried mud from the deep-tread tyres, emitting black smoke.

Renshaw spoke with contempt. 'He still on about that? Little Joey there. He didn't get beaten up. He got drunk, had to hold him down.' The foreman, Bradford, lumbered up to join the group. A crane swung a load of lumber across over their heads. 'You ask the foreman, there,' went on Renshaw. 'Ask any of the boys. Now if you're not official – and you're not here with my permission – we get a lot of pilfering, so we don't like strangers on the site, right?'

His belligerence was now marked, his face angry and his fists half cocked. Cowley nodded serenely.

'Really? We'll see the local constabulary look into that. Make sure your affairs are properly looked after in future. Isn't that so, Mr Halloran?' The tables had turned over quite nicely, thank you . . . 'Now,' said Cowley, 'we'd better let Mr Renshaw get back to his drawing boards.'

Halloran held his own anger in, joying in Cowley's verbal pyrotechnics. 'You're lucky it isn't mailbags.'

As Renshaw blinked at this, Cowley let one of his rare smiles curve his lips, taking all the harsh power-lines from his face and replacing them with lines of amusement. 'Oh, I wouldn't be certain of anyone's luck.'

Renshaw and Bradford stood together as Cowley and Halloran walked away. Both men were plug-uglies; but they recognised toughness when they met it.

'What's he after?' said Renshaw. He looked not as comfortable as he had been. 'We got the verdict behind us.'

Bradford provided the obvious answer. 'Councillor Webb?'

The site manager nodded, abruptly apprehensive.

The two C.I.5 agents waited for Halloran and the chief to join them. They recognised the spritely way Cowley walked, his limp absent, his sandy hair loose, the vigour in him.

'Bodie, Doyle – you will now mingle with the twelve good men and true of the Temple-Blake jury.'

Nodding, Bodie said: 'And you, sir?'

Cowley waited until a lorry trundled by with aggregate, some of it spilling past the rusty chains holding the drop sides in place. 'Remember the advice of my engineer friend who wanted – and not for the only time – to blow up a bridge. A lot of material going into that site. A lot of material – and a lot of paperwork. Some of it papering over the cracks. And one of them very close to an accountant, supposedly deceased of a self-administered dose of weedkiller.' He glared at Bodie. 'Not a typical way for an accountant to die. Or – would you say so, Bodie?'

He went off, not limping, heading for the white Rover 3500 and some more flat stones to turn over.

Halloran hitched up his shoulder, staring after Cowley.

'Don't think I'd like it much,' Halloran said, giving his honest opinion. 'If he got his teeth into me.'

'No,' said Doyle. 'You wouldn't.'

'Least you could expect,' amplified Bodie, 'would be a rare and fatal form of blood poisoning.'

The stable yard of Sir James Temple's palatial mansion was kept in scrupulously clean condition. Temple rather cared for horses – rather more than he did for most people, at any rate – and he was adamant that no unhygienic conditions would bring any of his prized specimens of horseflesh down. He pooh-poohed any comments about the cracked ceilings and damp walls of the houses his firm built, the fungus growing under the stairs, the electrical wiring like spaghetti, the breeding grounds of human diseases.

The white paint gleamed on the half-doors, the lichened tiles looked as though they would be chosen by an artist to represent the beauty of the English country house, the fire-extinguishers, bright red and functional, on their brackets denoted the way Temple liked it – the best of the old and the best of the new, tradition and efficiency.

He rode in now astride Beauty, who sweated from the workout, and that did not worry Sir James. He liked horses, yes; but he paid his grooms to take care of them, that was their job, and he'd dismiss instantly any one of them who fouled up. But a horse sweating after he had ridden her – well, that was mere routine. He dismounted and flung the reins at Johnson, the groom, and then walked off towards Logan-Blake.

Logan-Blake leaned against the whitewashed wall, looking amused. The expression was a mere façade. The moment he and Temple were out of earshot of the groom, Logan-Blake said: 'Repton says we have problems.'

'They must be his as well. Nothing else could drag him out of the financial canyons into the country.'

They walked across to Henry Repton. He looked harassed. He waited for them by a shiny limousine, and he reacted as the other two in their country clothes came up.

'Good morning, Henry,' said Sir James in his suave way. 'Glad you could come down. Perhaps you could join us for a few holes – ?'

'No, thank you, Sir James.' Repton looked distinctly unhappy now.

'Fresh air will do you good, Henry.'

Repton made a face. A groom came out of a stall and threw surgical dressings he had taken from a horse on to the small but efficient incinerator in the stable yard. The smoke wafted.

Repton said pointedly: 'Fresh air is something we might all be a bit short of, Sir James. For a very long time. Unless you've swept up after the Temple-Blake affair.' He nodded at the stable yard and the incinerator. 'As well as your grooms have swept up here. Carefully.'

'Oh, indeed,' said Sir James, lazily. 'Isn't that so, coz?'

'With clear consciences all around. The man in the wig said Not Guilty.'

'He had to.' Repton's expression had not changed.

'Thanks to the jury.' Logan-Blake looked smug at that.

'Cowley doesn't believe him. He's taking it very personally. Because he thinks he was gulled.'

'He was.' Sir James flicked his riding crop against his highly-polished boot. 'Very bright of him. Sorry you're not staying, Henry. The chauffeur will see you back to town.'

The two cousins strolled away. They left Repton by the large and shiny limousine. Suddenly, the sunshine was not as warm as it had been to the senior Civil Servant.

Aubrey Singleton, sociology lecturer in a dead-end career, finished packing his papers away in his briefcase. The blackboard was filled with diagrams and formulae. The classroom was empty – empty save for the still form of Bodie, who sat, chin propped on the back of the chair in front, watching Singleton.

'Were you waiting for someone?' said Singleton. He didn't recognise half of the dimwits he was supposed to teach.

Bodie shook his head.

Half-way down the aisle between the chairs Singleton paused again. 'Can I help?'

Again Bodie shook his head. He looked something like a quiescent Buddha – quiet and waiting – Singleton had the irrational thought he was like a wild animal waiting for prey.

Almost out through the door Singleton shocked to a standstill as Bodie's voice reached him. 'Mr Singleton!'

The words were perfectly ordinary; yet Aubrey Singleton froze in his tracks. He turned back, gripping his briefcase.

'Yes,' said Bodie. He stood up, and his eyebrows bent down fiercely upon Singleton. 'Yes, you can help. Or, to put it another way – I can help you.' He spoke now with forceful authority. 'Stop you going to jail, Aubrey. I can call you Aubrey, Aubrey?'

Singleton felt all his nightmares coalesce and overwhelm him. This he had feared. And, this, had happened . . .

Ray Doyle collected William Musgrave at the hardware shop as his ration. Doyle stood poking about among tins of paint. He walked over to Musgrave with a pair of paintbrushes in his hand. Doyle put on a puzzled expression.

'These any good for whitewash?'

'Yes – ' Musgrave looked as puzzled as Doyle; it was clear he didn't know one end of a brush from another to asked a damnfool question like that.

'Cover ups?' said Doyle. 'Snow jobs? Turning the proverbial blind eye?'

'What?'

Doyle put on his most sorrowful air. 'Did they pay you? Or put the frighteners on?'

'Who are you?' Musgrave's sour expression of defeat turned into one of indignation.

Doyle shook his head. 'Perverting the course of justice. Know that expression? Course you do. Thought you might. Got a nice quiet office where we can talk?' Musgrave hesitated; but he knew, as Singleton had known, what this was about. He started to lead the way to the office. Doyle went on musingly: 'Been talking to your wife. Off to Majorca, eh? Had a bit of a windfall . . . Been going to the dogs.'

Musgrave nodded. It was a story he had thought might –

Doyle smiled. 'Aren't we all?'

When Cowley called in to see Councillor Webb, the councillor had heard men were making awkward enquiries. As he and Cowley spoke he grew steadily more furious.

'There's nothing incriminating to find! Because Councillor Webb's done nothing to incriminate himself. Has he? A man's been tried and he's entitled to say that's that. You've had your game and the better man's won. You don't try him twice, not in the democratic society where I come from.'

'How long have you been associated with Tony Logan-Blake?'

'Tony who?' Webb blustered it out. 'Another one of your bloody double-barrelled aristos?'

'You don't know him?' Cowley looked interested.

''Course I know him. I know who he is, that's all. His friends are on the other side of the Council. Not mine. And before you say anything, let me say something. That judge said we could go. And that means Councillor Webb's innocent. His friends out there who are buying him drinks say so, too. So if you want to say any more, you'd better start thinking. I've got my lawyers, too.'

'Good.' Cowley nodded briskly. He had watched the performance with keen interest. 'Perhaps you'd better bring them with you. Oh – did no one tell you? The Director of Public Prosecutions is considering an enquiry. Into this question of suborning jurors. Purely a formality in your case.' Cowley could see where his words were hurting. 'I'm sure we'll find someone who is guilty.'

Cowley smiled again and walked gently away. Councillor Webb stared after him. He was aware his mouth hung open foolishly; but he felt so sick he could not even shut his mouth.

Sipping iced tea on the lawns of his stately home was a far more pleasant way to spend life than, for instance, working on a building site or living in a rat-trap living-unit his firm had put up, and Sir James Temple was a man who relished the good things of life. He could afford them. His fellow workers worked well, and Sir James reaped the rewards. A manservant brought the phone out with its lead stretching back to the french windows, and Temple took the call. He listened and his expression did not alter. Logan-Blake, watching from the other side of the table, waited.

When Temple had finished the phone was removed, and he said to his cousin: 'That was our friendly police Super.'

'The one with the all too young and expensive wife?'

Sir James smiled. 'He did sound a little weary.'

'Enviable . . . '

Sir James spoke evenly; but there was an edge under the suave words. 'Word has come down C.I.5 are investigating the jury on the corruption case. Headed by our human mole, Cowley.'

He stood up and walked a little way along the terrace. He was not entirely convinced everything was as spick-and-span as he would wish, despite Logan-Blake's calm assurances. He turned back.

'So we are sure, cousin?'

'Very. Confident.' Logan-Blake did not stir from his seat. 'If any of the jurors do talk, what will they find?' He gestured negligently, sweeping the problem away. 'A frightened sociology teacher? A greedy store deputy manager? You know who they are?'

'No. Never heard of them.'

'More important, coz – ' And here Logan-Blake smiled that lazy, self-confident smile. 'They've never heard of you – or me.'

Sir James nodded. 'So we can say – no loose ends. You're confident.' Logan-Blake waved his hand again, assured. Sir James went on: 'Do you remember how careful Bobby Gillam was?'

'Indeed.' It was a standing joke – rather, it had been a standing joke. 'Not one but two spare pairs of shoe-laces in his briefcase. And an extra stiff collar.'

'I spent the entire day going through the executive offices.'

'Looking for the private accounts?' Logan-Blake checked his knowing smile. 'I told you where they were. In the boardroom safe. I checked them myself.'

'And,' said Sir James with that check of indrawn breath. 'You've been through Gillam's papers?'

'Yes. I wish I had his secretary. Mine does the filing like a combine harvester.' And, still, Logan-Blake had no idea of the direction Sir James was leading. His confidence was absolute.

'And you didn't find this.' Sir James handed across a pale-pink slip of paper. 'Requisition for three hundred sheets of photocopying paper?' Logan-Blake looked at the pink slip without visible change of expression. Sir James drew his breath, again, and spoke in just the same suave way. 'I see it means nothing to you. Dear old Bobby – ' Logan-Blake got the venomous sarcasm in that, well enough. ' – the tidy mind, meticulous to the last, accounting for everything – tips to cloakroom attendants – and three hundred sheets of photocopying paper – '

Logan-Blake sat up. His smooth full-fleshed face looked abruptly cautious. 'The private accounts.' He looked up at his cousin. 'Robert copied them before he caught bellyache. Dear, sweet, cautious Robert. What pointed you at that?'

'You, coz. Because you're the sharp one. The one we take out insurance against. Every private paper that's gone through that boardroom safe has also been photocopied by me. And I'm not as bright as you or Gillam – was. I simply have the same regard for insuring my own skin – and my overseas bank accounts.' He spoke directly now, a question and an order. 'Loose end?'

'I hope not . . . '

'Hope is for the underprivileged. And they're rather overcrowded. Why add us?' His aplomb still existed as a tangible force. This could not dent his composure, not yet, because he was Sir James Temple. 'I'm sorry,' he said, as Logan-Blake rose, somewhat hurriedly, 'I'm sorry you have to rush back to town.'

Burton, the juror on the Temple-Blake corruption case who lived on the Fairgrove Estate, was contacted by Cowley. Some of the disgusting results of shoddy workmanship and adulterated building materials were clearly in evidence as they toured the house. Other results would turn up, years later, in the hospitals. There had been no attempt to bribe Burton, as he said, cynically, not with a Temple-Blake address. The jury, he said, had been led and it had been a case of follow my leader.

Cowley's feelings at the disgusting state of the building this man and his wife and child were expected to inhabit in this day and age in a democratic sovereign country were those of a man confronted with an offensive smell in a rose-garden. And this was no isolated case. The less fortunate folk of these islands were being done down, done down rotten – and leave aside perfectly truthful talk of lazy layabouts who wouldn't work if you offered it to them – and no amount of glossy advertising and top-of-the-head romantic trash could cover up the stink.

C.I.5 had been set up to combat crime. That this involved hectic car chases, and gun battles, and clever forensic medicine, and all the rest of the high-powered way of life of the Big A's squad of tearaways in the cause of justice, could not detract from the honest-to-God truth that in this situation, here and now, in this slice of real life, C.I.5 were fighting crime. Fighting crime of a particularly nasty, underhand, vicious character.

'You paint a very clear picture,' said Cowley as they went through the hall where the nice new wallpaper Burton had hung two months ago now peeled away with leprous patches and the colours all faded. 'Have you been on many juries?'

'No. But I've been a works convenor. And I've sat on a lot of committees where the votes have been settled up front and favours are being paid off. Somebody had told enough people on that jury what to do. And they did it, believe me.'

They went out through the doorway where the door made its usual creak on opening, and would never close properly, and Cowley saw Doyle's white Escort just drawing up. He put the question he had to put, with those emotions of disgust in him.

'And if we ever got near making a case of this, would you talk?'

Burton rubbed a limp fist over his forehead. He knew

the score, for he lived in the real world. 'I doubt it. I'm a council tenant, aren't I? It may not be much and getting a council house is difficult; but it is my home. Sorry . . . '

The gate of the little cracked-concrete path did not fall off as they went out; but it would, soon, and Burton would have to put in fresh hinges. If all the problems of the houses could be settled as simply, there'd be no problem. Doyle came across and said at once: 'They've spirited Gillam's widow away. Off to a health farm.'

'Have they now?' said Cowley, feeling pleased.

'And all a bit quick.'

'They want Gillam's house empty.' Cowley felt the itch in his nose, and did not feel the bullet in his leg. Life was suddenly looking up. He turned away from the sad little council house and went towards his car. 'The rats,' he told Doyle, 'are coming out of their holes to take the cheese.'

The partners worked the old one-two act with Bodie making an expert and silent break-in to Gillam's house and Doyle in the little tent rigged up beside the yellow Post Office van. Doyle looked like an honest workman, which made Bodie smile. And Bodie acted like a burglar, which made Doyle smile.

From the tent Doyle kept observation on the gateway and drive and road beyond. Bodie maintained communication with him over the walkie-talkie in clipped, laconic half-sentences.

The two settled down to watch and wait.

Bodie checked the empty house, seeing evidences of the luxuries Gillam's ill-gotten gains had bought. He eased open the curtains partially-closed over the upstairs windows and looked out to Doyle's yellow van and tent.

All Bodie knew, from the rapid briefing Cowley had given him, was that they – whoever 'they' turned out to be – would be looking for papers that would incriminate the big-wigs. As he put it: 'They'll be looking for the papers mentioned by a Colonel who was at the Relief of Mafeking.'

Doyle's voice came in over the R./T:

'Vanish. They're here.'

They were confident. The house was empty – they knew that. A pick-up truck openly marked with the bold block lettering: TEMPLE-BLAKE LTD drove up along the drive and Renshaw got out. He looked about, dark and hard, and then went to the door. A Mercedes sports car nosed into the drive and drew up alongside the pick-up. Karl Drake alighted and joined Renshaw. Both men entered the house.

Into his walkie-talkie, Bodie said: 'Recognise 'em?'

'One,' said Doyle from the tent. 'And the other's no powder puff.'

Bodie, too, had recognised the strength and lethality of the man with Renshaw. But, being Bodie, he had to say: 'Soft as marshmallow. Don't go away. Might need you.'

Keeping low and well out of sight, Bodie took full advantage of the shadows in the house where the drawn curtains threw umber sombreness over the antique furniture and darkly-glimmering brasses, the polished balustrade. He checked the progress of the two below.

Renshaw looked around the house and his face expressed his awareness of where it was at. 'Did himself proud. We do the labouring, they own the racehorses. Perhaps – ' said Renshaw with a sidelong look at Drake. 'Perhaps, if we find the papers, we could win ourselves a racehorse each.' His face twisted at his thoughts. 'Keep them – 'til they hand over.'

Drake's words were those of the cold professional who knew the score so much better than these amateurs. 'Don't think about finding them, friend. Just worry about what will happen to you if we don't find them.'

Renshaw licked his lips. Toughness in the pub and building site he understood. But this man wore an aura of toughness quite outside Renshaw's colourful experience.

Watching them from his concealing shadows, Bodie saw the way they went about the search. They turned the place over. He kept out of their way, skilfully, and presently they stood once again in the hall below. Bodie peered through the banisters. He held the walkie-talkie close to his mouth, whispering so that Doyle could just read him.

'Can't say he's an amateur. He knows where to look . . .'

The men below went into the library again and Renshaw threw the desk drawer on to the carpet. The movement was pettish. 'Nothing. These intellectual snobs. Everything in its place – except what we're looking for.'

Drake was sardonic. 'Three copies of his will. You know where he topped himself, had that last one for the road?'

'Greenhouse?'

'Greenhouse. Where a man goes to drink – and die – a careful man.'

Renshaw kicked the drawer away and followed Drake out. Bodie eased down the stairs and said to Doyle: 'Greenhouse – on our way.'

The flowers gave forth their scents in an almost solid bank of sweet aromas. The colours fired with beauty. The greenhouse presented the appearance of a pleasure palace filled with delights. Karl Drake looked about, a hunter on the scent of prey.

'It's about being hurt or wounded in rough country. An instinct tells you where to hole up. Animal. Refuge . . .' He saw the place where Gillam had died, the potting bench, the sink and taps, the cupboard. 'He'd want to keep the papers dry. Where would we find the heating system for this funeral parlour?'

The small greenhouse heater with its thermostatic controls maintaining even temperature purred gently to itself. Renshaw moved across and flipped the slatted lid up.

'This what you're looking for?' He reached in and took out a brown paper parcel, rectangular, with sharp corners, sealed with Sellotape. 'Doesn't look like it's worth much.'

Drake's answering smile chilled. 'Not even a racehorse each? Could keep you out of jail, that. How much is that worth?'

Drake took the parcel and placed it on the bench. He reached up and opened the cupboard, took out the bottle of

Bell's. The level hadn't changed much. He unscrewed the top and took a swig. Renshaw eyed him.

'You know your way around this place, don't you?'

'I wouldn't let that trouble you.' Drake took the bottle away from his lips with a glug and a splash. 'Or – maybe it should. You weren't really serious about double dealing our masters – were you?'

Things added up for Renshaw – sudden and ugly things. He felt shaken. 'No – not really. Just thought you might – '

Drake shook his head. His smile might have come off an ice floe out of Spitzbergen.

Moving at high speed, Bodie catapulted out of the other arm of the greenhouse. He was intent on that all-important brown-paper parcel. He chopped at Drake who swerved, sending plant pots flying, and kicked back. Bodie grabbed for the parcel and ducked to evade the blow from Renshaw. He only half avoided the attack and reeled away, scattering more flowers and smashing pots. Drake scooped the parcel and ran as Renshaw hit Bodie again. Bodie sprawled over. Drake raced outside.

Sprawled on the floor, seeing everything through a distorted mist, Bodie saw Renshaw run past. Bodie grabbed an ankle. As the site manager tripped forward, Bodie had just enough strength to turn the trip into a throw. Renshaw slammed forward. His dark head hit the brick coping. There was a soggy thump. Renshaw lay still.

Bodie knew he shouldn't shake his head; but he did so, anyway, and amid the clangour of fireballs felt some senses returning. He got a knee under him and forced himself to rise. After a bit he took out his handcuffs and cuffed Renshaw to the waterpipe against the glass. Then he staggered outside.

He was just in time to see Doyle revving the yellow van across the drive. Drake was gunning his Merc down the drive, the engine howling and the tyres spitting gravel. Drake saw the little yellow van blocking the drive. Without hesitation he twisted the wheel and shot past the Post Office van, smashed through the white-painted fencing out across the pavement and into the road. With the accelerator flat to the floorboards he roared away.

Doyle watched him go – and smiled.

Bodie rolled up, his face wrathful.

'You,' Bodie told his partner. 'Couldn't stop a fat lady in a thin alley.'

Doyle, still smiling, rather cared for Bodie's vivid descriptive flair. He reached down and hauled out the R./T. He spoke jauntily.

'He's on his way.'

Bodie glared, simmering. 'You let him go!'

Doyle nodded. 'What d'you want me to do? Chase him? In this?' He opened the passenger door. 'We'd catch him in 1980, or when he runs out of petrol. Get in.'

Feeling old, Bodie got in.

Flames from the stable yard incinerator rose, lacy and orange, into the sunshine. Johnson fed the rest of the soiled surgical dressings into the flames. Sir James Temple looked with a pensiveness on Sir Lancelot, and patted his sleek neck. The horse's new bandages stood out starkly on his near foreleg, and he wouldn't put that hoof to the ground for a long time.

'Don't know what to do about you, old chap.' Sir James patted the horse's neck again, thinking. 'We've all got to earn our keep.'

The incinerator smelled unpleasantly, and Temple moved a little way off, with a last look at Sir Lancelot. As he turned to leave the stable yard he saw the low-slung Mercedes draw up beyond the white-painted picket fence and Drake get out. The hard man came over, moving with determination. Temple's features composed themselves at their most languid.

'Wins nothing,' he said, carrying on the conversation with the horse and transferring it to Drake. 'Ought to sell the wretched beast.'

He was fully aware of the brown-paper parcel under Drake's arm. Now, easily, he reached for it. 'Is that for me?'

It was done smoothly, a mere matter of tiresome routine. Drake shifted the parcel away and Temple's wrinkled hand fell short.

'Tell me,' said Drake, and the viciousness in his words was not lost on Sir James Temple. 'Tell me about the goons organising the welcome committee.'

'I didn't know.' Temple favoured him with a shifty, sideways glance. 'Well, you're a man of resource. There'll be a bonus for you. Say – five hundred.'

Again he reached for the parcel.

Drake said: 'Say five thousand.'

There was no perceptible hesitation as Temple nodded. They walked out of the shadows of the stableyard together. The business they concluded in Temple's polished study satisfied them both. Temple took the parcel. Drake put the fat envelope with the five thousand into his pocket. They went out on to the terrace and saw the white Rover 3500 pulling up along the drive. Temple moved easily.

'Visitors. Perhaps you could make your own discreet way out. I don't think we need receipts.'

Drake moved away, agreeing, and waited until the man alighted from the white Rover. The Mercedes was parked just beyond. The man from the Rover looked at the Merc and then started off towards the house. Waiting until he was out of sight, Karl Drake started off for his own car.

Cowley saw Sir James Temple moving swiftly towards the stable yard. He followed up, going quietly over the paving stones. The incinerator flamed up, still burning fiercely. Temple pulled the parcel out from under his arm and held it out over the flames – and Cowley's voice reached him like the blow from a cleaver.

'I'll take the parcel, Sir James.'

Temple swung about, his face still assured and contemptuous.

'We have a warrant do we?'

'No,' said Cowley. 'But we do know where that comes from and what it contains.'

Sir James Temple hadn't got where he was today by

being slow. He thrust forward ready to throw the incriminating photocopied evidence into the flames. Cowley seized his arm, grabbing for the parcel, and the two men struggled for only a moment. Cowley dismissed Temple with ease, sent him staggering back. But he still had the parcel and he saw over Cowley's shoulder the tall, ominous form of Karl Drake approaching at a run.

'Ashes to ashes,' said Temple. 'And do what we must.'

As Drake grabbed Cowley, intending to chuck the old buffer in an insensible heap to the flagstones, Temple made a last and successful dash for the flames. The parcel went in. The fire ate hungrily at the brown paper wrappings.

Cowley broke free from Drake with a body-twisting turn, got an elbow in, staggered back from a vicious blow that he only just managed to change from a haymaker to his chin to a stinging buffet on his shoulder. Drake bored in, and if he killed the old fool he wouldn't care.

Cowley stumbled back against the wall. A red blur in the corner of his eye . . . He reached up, ripped the fire-extinguisher free and triggered a quick burst that covered Drake's head and shoulders with foam.

The man stumbled back, yelling, clawing at his face.

Temple rushed up to give Cowley a push. As Cowley fell, off-balance, Drake got his eyes free. He turned as the sound of a car engine reached into the stable yard. A little yellow Post Office van trundled up. Bodie and Doyle leaped out.

With a yell of anger, Drake hared off, evading Bodie.

'Yours – ' called Bodie.

'Thank you,' said Doyle, most precisely. He drop-kicked Drake where it would do the most good and as the man went down, jumped on him. He started to haul out the handcuffs.

'Thanks, Joe,' he said. 'One to go.'

Sir James had lost all his aristocratic cool. Red murder flamed in his head. He charged at Cowley again. The C.I.5 chief managed to swing the fire extinguisher around in a clumsy arc and crashed the red-painted cylinder into Temple's shins.

Temple toppled, yelling in agony. Bodie stepped across him and took the fire extinguisher from Cowley, who looked like a big game hunter still wreathed in powder smoke.

'Ole,' said Bodie. He spoke admiringly. That was for Cowley. But they looked at the burning parcel in the incinerator. 'Ole,' said Bodie, glumly.

'Never mind, Bodie.' Cowley stood up and pulled his jacket straight. 'Let it burn. The real parcel with the copy accounts is already on its way to the Fraud Squad. We only needed to prove who needed them and to what lengths and to what address they'd go.'

Temple brushed his coat lapels down, removing the dust. He looked – how did one look, Bodie wondered, in moments like this? Sir James Temple looked sullen and savage and – and just a little frightened?

'Ashes to ashes – dust to dust,' said Cowley, brushing his own lapels. 'I look forward to meeting your lawyers in court, Sir James. And young Mr Logan-Blake.'

Bodie, Doyle and Cowley looked at one another. The fire blazed up in the incinerator. But, this time, flames had not destroyed everything they touched.

The sacred sanctum of the senior Civil Servant contained Henry Repton and the Minister, both at the shining desk, when Cowley came in. He looked at them with cold dislike. The wheels had moved, the weights had fallen and the mills were even now grinding. When they had finished the resultant pieces would be small – very small indeed.

'I've been instructed by my own Minister to convey to you the contents of a report which he will lay before Cabinet.' Cowley spoke evenly, his modulated accents plummy as usual. But there was no mistaking the disgust he felt. 'The Fraud Squad analysis has disclosed that one of your senior Civil Servants has been actively engaged in corruption for some years. He may wish to resign before going to court.' Cowley did not look at Repton; he kept his hard gaze fixed on the Minister. 'The trivial case, which was the cause of our being brought into this affair, will be retried and with it will be a separate murder charge.'

The Minister opened his mouth, closed it, opened it again to say a little breathlessly: 'Are you saying I had any idea this was happening when I called you in?'

'I am saying only that you sought to use my Department for personal and political ends and I will not tolerate that.'

'All the arrogance there is.' The Minister sat back in his chair, his colour high, a tremble in his lips, his whole stance that of a man who has been suddenly pushed back. 'Hound, judge, then jury.'

'No, Minister.' Cowley shook his head. 'Rule of law. I am not here in this office of my own volition. I am playing your rules of what passes for courtesy in the corridors of power.'

'And what do you suggest I do?'

Cowley said at once: 'Resign.' Then his contempt broke out as he went on: 'But we live in a world without much honour and where politicians hang on to office like dirty glue, so I don't suppose you will. Blame is for others.'

Cowley stood up. He nodded curtly at them. They could feel his distaste for them and their ways. He went out and there was a silence for some time in that plush and sacred sanctum.

Then Repton spoke. He spoke tentatively, beginning to work on his life again. He said: 'Minister . . . '

That was as far as Henry Repton, senior Civil Servant, reached. The Minister got up and without a word went out of the office.

The weights dropped and the gears turned and the mills ground. It all took time. But, in the end, what justice could be meted out was meted out. Cowley accosted Bodie and Doyle as they came out of the Fraud Squad's offices. He looked pointedly at his wristwatch.

'You're spending a lot of time talking to this Fraud Squad man, Riordan, is it?'

'He's good,' said Bodie. 'Says the deadliest crossfire's

between two sets of balance sheets when the fingers on the pens are crooked.'

'And,' said Doyle. 'The most efficient blunt instrument is a cheque book with money in the bank behind it.'

'You two are really branching out.'

But all three knew that this Temple-Blake affair had put them in touch with the real world, the real world out there beyond Whitehall, where men and women struggled to make an honest living, and worried about the cost of everything, and were done down, done down rotten, all day and every day.

Cowley nodded. 'Don't try putting the drinks on your expenses though?'

'Why?' Doyle screwed up his eyes and spoke a trifle tartly. 'It's work.'

Cowley turned his lined, shrewd face towards Doyle. 'Sounds more like education. And education's never free.'

Chapter Seven

The rain that morning had spread a shining slick of water over the rusty corrugated iron and crumbled brickwork. The water shone in puddles in the pot-holed road, narrow and confining, between the tall warehouse walls. Most of the oblong Victorian windows were boarded up; a few still had incongruous window-panes, the glass thick with streaked mud. The spiders were cautiously coming out and surveying their kingdoms, repairing their webs and getting set for the day's business of catching flies.

The large black limousine rolled slowly along the narrow street. Its black polish shone as the sun strove to break through the vanishing clouds. The day would be bright.

The car stopped opposite a sagging doorway and two men alighted. They were large, bulky men, moving with purpose. Their blue suits were of a solid yet un-English cut. They stared at the serried ranks of blank windows, their square, pale faces expressing only a perfunctory interest. This meet was routine.

The third man alighted. He moved briskly and yet with the same sense of heaviness of purpose as his aides. This was Comrade Colonel Grigor Yashinkov, his cover a military attaché, his function – a K.G.B. Controller. He went swiftly into the abandoned warehouse. His aides followed, their hands in their coat pockets.

When they had gone the man at the high window opposite moved a little forward, stared down, and spoke quietly into his walkie-talkie.

Yashinkov and his aides went up to the second storey. The warehouse stretched about them like a looted cathedral. The dust lay in windows. The cobwebs clustered in the corners. The shafts of strengthening sunlight lay in long ordered rows from the rectangular windows, making the wide room a shadowed sunlight-barred cavern. Yashinkov and his aides moved towards the far end, and then, as his aides halted, the Colonel moved on alone. He stopped, waiting quietly.

The silhouette of the man standing waiting for him moved against the light of the end window. The black silhouette turned and stepped forward a few paces. The whole scene held undertones of menace, of ill-will, of a deadly waiting quietness. These men were not playing games – and yet, and yet, as George Cowley stepped up to greet the Comrade Colonel he knew somewhat sourly that this was all a make-believe. It was a routine farce. He and Yashinkov could just as easily meet in a restaurant somewhere, but the Russians liked it this way. The cloak-and-dagger stuff was, to Cowley, and to Bodie and Doyle who now stepped at his back, complementing the aides across from them, very much passé.

'Hello, Comrade,' said Cowley.

'Hello, tovarich,' said Yashinkov.

'The rest of the K.G.B. listening in, Grigor?'

'This is an arrangement of trust,' said the K.G.B. man. 'Based on trust, tovarich. Mutual trust. The K.G.B. respects such a trust.'

Over the narrow street the man with the walkie-talkie in the glassless window connected it up to his cassette recorder. It was a matter of trust; but C.I.5 would have that trust down on tape – just as the K.G.B. would.

A few trivial routine matters were disposed of first.

Cowley was saying: 'Skopshlev is becoming an embarrassment to M.I.6, Grigor. They'll have to jump him soon. He's too obvious. And he's run up some hefty bills still outstanding in Soho . . . '

'Third Secretary Skopshlev will be sent back to Moscow immediately.'

'Aye. Otherwise we'll have the C.I.A. poking their noses in.'

Bodie and Doyle were right turned off by this. 'What a circus,' said Bodie, with great disgust. 'All dust and shadows. Like something out of *The Third Man*.'

'Tuesday,' said Doyle, low, so that their voices did not carry. 'Last week. Late night movie on the box.'

'Yeah.' Bodie hitched his immaculate suit up. 'Well, maybe that was the scene in Berlin thirty years ago – but this is the middle of bloody London.' He twitched his nostrils fiercely 'Dust gets right up my hooter. Plays hell with my sinuses.'

'It was Vienna,' Doyle told his partner, resigned. 'Orson Wells and Joseph Cotten.'

'Who was the bird?'

'Valli. Alida Valli.'

'Was she stacked?'

Doyle sighed. 'You're a moron.'

Cowley was carefully disseminating information. 'And they're bringing back Rashid from Cairo. That leaves only four on the South Med Station.' He paused. 'That's about the lot. What have you got for me?'

Yashinkov looked apologetic. 'Very little, I'm afraid. A very quiet period – '

'It's never been a very quiet period, Grigor.'

'I am sending Boris Kirilsky into the field.'

Cowley held back his impatience. 'You told me that at our last meeting. I've had him tabbed for ten days.'

'He is not important. You can pick him up, if you want.'

'This is all one-way traffic!'

Cowley glared at the K.G.B. man.

Yashinkov said: 'A British Trade Delegate lost his passport in Moscow five days ago.'

With great but still partially controlled exasperation, Cowley said: 'I can get that sort of information from F.O. circulars.'

'We think it may have been stolen,' Yashinkov went on steadily. 'We are having the hotel staff interrogated.' He eyed Cowley there in the shadows and the dust. 'His name is Williams. George Henry Williams.'

Cowley shook his head. 'It's the same every time, Yashinkov! I pass you good stuff – and I get rubbish in return.'

Yashinkov spread his hands like a horse trader on the steppes of Central Mother Russia. 'Ask me for something, tovarich. Anything. Mutual trust . . .'

Cowley grunted in disbelieving disgust. He turned away – and then he swung back. He took a step forward. He looked hard at the Russian. Cunning. George Cowley, cunning and brilliant and lethal.

'All right,' he said. 'Moscow.' A fraction of a second passed and then, in a higher voice, he said: 'And Thomas Darby.'

The atmosphere in the eerie deserted warehouse chilled abruptly. Yashinkov's hard square face tightened up. His two aides stiffened.

'Hello, hello . . .' said Bodie, suddenly interested.

In a hushed voice, Doyle whispered: 'Talking of the Third bloody Man . . .'

The silence stretched. The sunlight dimmed as a cloud passed. The dust lay in heavy swathes. Yashinkov took a step towards Cowley and lowered his voice. 'Darby?'

'Thomas Darby. One of our old Judases.'

'Ghosts? You want to know about ghosts, tovarich? What can I tell you – you don't know already, eh? He has been a Soviet citizen for the past twenty years or more. He lives quietly in Moscow. He is inactive. He is retired –'

'And no one has seen him for some days. He's dropped out of sight.'

'A sick, tired old man. I have heard nothing. All I know is that he is ill.'

'Our people say he is no longer in Moscow. So where is he?'

Yashinkov held out his arms. 'All right – so Thomas Darby is dying. Perhaps he has only a few months left. When it happens you will read his obituary in *Pravda.*'

Doggedly, Cowley said: 'He is not in Moscow.'

'Do your agents know more than the K.G.B., tovarich?'

There was no answer to that – at least, no answer Cowley was prepared to give. 'Snow job,' he said, well-knowing the Russian would understand his meaning.

Yashinkov shook his head, anxious now to terminate this meeting.

'If there is nothing else . . . ?'

Now the signing-off routine could be gone through with still formal protocol, harking back to crinkling black and white films in the archives, memories of the Wall and the dusty blowing wind, and spies, and all the paraphernalia of an apparat extending into this modern world. Yashinkov's two aides stepped up to his side, flanking him, and Bodie and Doyle flanked Cowley. The first Aide smiled – a gruesome grimace – and shook hands with Doyle.

'Up the workers, eh?' said Doyle.

The other Aide shook with Bodie.

Bodie said, straight-faced, smooth, half-smiling: 'Arsenal for the Cup.'

The Aide said: 'Da.'

The pantomime over, they parted. Yashinkov said: 'Until the next time, tovarich.' The three K.G.B. men turned, all in unison, like clockwork marionettes, and marched away into the shadows. When they had gone Cowley stood, thinking deep thoughts, in the sunlight through a window. Dust motes danced.

Bodie sneezed.

In a low voice, Doyle said: 'Gesundheit, tovarich.'

'Bloody Ivans.' Bodie was disgusted, right choked. 'I knew it. Right up the hooter.'

'Wonder what the K.G.B. rates of pay are like?'

'Grim.' Doyle sounded assured. 'They do it all for Mother Russia.'

'Then they're crazier than we are.'

After a time they went out to the narrow street. Cowley checked the old story of Tom Darby with them. Furnell, McNaught and Darby, the arch defectors – twenty years ago. Furnell was dead, McNaught was insane – and Darby, the big one, had been a Colonel, K.G.B. undercover. Double Agent. Top man in S.I.S., defected from Syria, and all hell broke loose. He'd blown up half a dozen networks. And now, as Cowley said, waiting for Lewis to bring the car up: 'Darby's left Moscow.'

Lewis, the man in the window opposite with the walkie-talkie and the cassette recorder, tooled an inconspicuous old Jaguar up and the three men got in.

'A dying man,' went on Cowley. 'But he still hankers after the wine and roses. *Or something*. He's on the run. And he's carrying a British passport under the name of Williams.'

'So where is Darby running to?' said Bodie.

'Where do you think?'

'Here?' Bodie sounded incredulous. 'Why leave a comfortable berth in Moscow to return to the land where – no way!'

'He has nowhere else to go, Bodie.'

'Yashinkov told you all that?'

'More or less, Bodie, more or less. He brought the subject around to Moscow. He wanted to make sure I knew about Darby. Right. Bodie, have C.I. make copies of the latest photo of Thomas Darby they have on file. Issue them to every member of the Squad. And when you get yours – study it. Get to know every line on Darby's face.'

Using the car radiophone, Cowley began the investigation. There was something here, his nose itch told him that. He found out very quickly that George Henry Williams had entered the country through Dover. He was not tagged. He was free and loose. And, he was dying.

Cowley put a clampdown on press releases. He looked grim as he put the phone down. Bodie raised his Bodie eyebrows.

'For one tired old spy?'

Cowley retorted with heat. 'That tired old spy could topple a government, start a fair old massacre – and bring a lot of maggots crawling out of the woodwork.'

'Well,' said Doyle, with a glance at Cowley. 'I suppose he's an embarrassment to Yashinkov and the K.G.B. They'd want him back . . . '

'Or they'd want him dead,' snapped Cowley. 'And there's a handful of ex-S.I.S. men, agents he blew-up, people with long and ugly memories. They'd be after his blood.' He tapped the phone. 'And there's the Fourth Man. Aye, the Fourth Man.'

'Who,' said Doyle, 'is he?'

'They've made a dozen guesses.' Cowley shook his head. 'Maybe all wrong. A lot of speculation – nothing positive. *The Banker*. The fellow who stayed behind. The fellow who financed everything, thought to be rich, influential, pillar of the Establishment. Powerful. Respectable. Keeping his secret from everyone – and – *still here*! He oiled the cogs for the three of them – twenty years ago – and with good clean money. He underwrote every operation, every payoff, every expense, to the tune of hundred of thousands of pounds.'

Bodie screwed around in the seat. 'And Darby knows who he is?' He pursed up his lips in a silent whistle.

'Right.'

'Which means that even if Darby wasn't dying,' Doyle pointed out. 'His life wouldn't be worth a bent penny.'

Cowley sat back. This was the core of it. 'Right again. And, personally, I don't care. But we still have to find him before anyone else does. Because I want to know why the hell he's taken it into his head to come back!' Cowley's words were taut with all the professional instincts of a master hunter faced with a master double agent. 'And I want to know who the Fourth Man is!'

In pursuance of those aims so laudable to a proper functioning of the services of the country, Cowley stirred up another ghost from the past. He arranged a meeting with Brigadier Stadden. If anyone knew anything, Stadden would. He had headed up S.I.S., had employed Tom Darby, and had seen his organisation blown sky-high when Darby defected. Now, of course, Stadden was long retired. He lived in one of those apparently stuffy red-brick mansions in St James's, where any luxury might be had, because only people with worldly wealth ever set foot there as owners. Stadden's study was book-lined, red and gold and brown, carpeted with a deep Oriental pile, lit with subdued taste. Now the lights were off and a slide-projector threw into flickering life on the screen more ghosts from the past.

Cowley spoke from the memoranda Stadden had prepared. His words were matched by the images flashed up on the screen.

'Sir Howell Mortimer, Stockbroker . . . ' As the black-and-white photographs flicked up on to the screen, Cowley went on with the description of Mortimer as a man with many contacts with Darby before his defection. Then the pictures changed. A hidden camera had caught Eileen Pierce in various places, mostly dull suburban streets. She was, in the pictures, just coming up to middle-age, gentle-faced, attractive. Cowley read out the statistics that matched the array of pictures.

'Mrs Eileen Pierce, widow. Her husband was killed in the Spanish Civil War fighting with the International Brigade.' Well, if anyone would know about that and about those days, George Cowley would. He rubbed his leg where the damned bullet lodged, and went on reading. 'He was politically active, but there was nothing on her. Believed to be a distant cousin of Darby's – but there's a query against that. She saw a lot of him in the years up to his defection. Said to be living in Highgate now. Address is on file.'

The next face from the past flashed up on the screen as the file on the Right Honourable Paul Cantwell was divulged. 'Land and property owner,' said Cowley. 'Millionaire. Was at University at the same time as Darby. Had a lot to do with him then.' Cantwell's pictures showed him against a Westminster background. He looked tall and elegant, full-fleshed, a man who had received more than his fair share of the country's wealth.

'Arthur Pulford,' read Cowley as the next sequence of old photographs flickered into life. 'Solicitor. Saw little of Darby; but was his lawyer and also the lawyer of Eileen Pierce. Still practices. Nothing else known.'

The last dossier of pictures showed a man of that bristling, military type who dominated his surroundings. He appeared in these archives from the past mostly in civvies; but one shot showed him in khaki and Sam Browne, the crown and three stars on his shoulder straps.

'Brigadier James Bernard Stadden, known as Brigadier S. Latterly Controller S.I.S. Head of Section Four.' Cowley looked up from the notes and stared in the dim lighting reflections at the wheelchair in which Stadden sat, shrunken, but still, after twenty years, with much of the old bristle about him. 'It was Brigadier Stadden who recruited Tom Darby into the S.I.S. in 1942. Remained as his immediate superior up until Darby's defection. Officially retired; but believed still alive as Consultant to Counter Intelligence Sections.'

As the lights went up Cowley admitted to himself that he admired that insouciant 'believed still alive'. Doyle who had been running the projector stilled it so that a big blow-up of Darby's face remained on the screen.

Stadden might be shrunken in body; but his face was still heavy and large, the features pronounced, the nose prominent, the lips wide. He had been a powerful Rugger man in his day. Now he cocked his bristly eyebrows as Cowley came over.

'One of them is the Banker. The Fourth Man.' Cowley spoke evenly. 'You included yourself in the list of suspects.'

'Of course.' Stadden's voice had a way of rolling the words around as though he was eating grapes. 'Some of my colleagues thought – still think – it's me. The files had to be complete. D'you think it's me, Cowley?'

'No.'

Stadden sighed. 'Of all the people in London Darby would keep farthest from – it's me. When he defected he left my Section in shreds. He destroyed a lot of good men. Yes, I'd kill him, I suppose – but for other reasons.'

'You must have a favourite amongst this lot. Politician, Stockbroker, Lawyer. I need to know, Brigadier. Darby's floating around somewhere and if the Banker gets to him –'

'Fool!' Stadden said in his heavy snorting way. 'Should have stayed in Moscow. Sentimentality is a mortal handicap for spies.'

'Sentimentality?' Cowley knew he had to humour the old boy. He had been brilliant in his time – the spark was still there.

'Anyway, those files are not up to date. Eileen Pierce is dead. She died last Tuesday week. Natural causes.'

His chuckle sounded like a sewer emptying. 'I still keep my finger on the pulse, you know.'

Cowley looked up. Doyle saw the flash of triumph cross the chief's face.

'That's ten days ago! Darby was still in Moscow. Darby came back because Eileen Pierce died! Who was she?'

Stadden let them have a death's head grin. 'Not the Banker. And not Darby's cousin, either.' He was enjoying tantalising them, these young whipper-snappers in the great game.

'Mistress?' demanded Cowley.

'Lovely old-fashioned turn of phrase, isn't it? Darby was human. She was very attractive. He knew her husband. Met him in Spain. Politically naïve.'

'Darby wouldn't come back just to mourn at Eileen Pierce's grave!'

Stadden coughed and grunted. 'Sentimentality.'

'Not enough.' Cowley was on to it and wasn't going to let go.

'Together,' said Stadden, acting it up to the hilt. 'They

compounded an unforeseen mistake. They had a child. Occupational hazard for mistresses before the Pill. Baby girl, some twenty or more years ago. Name of Helen Pierce.'

Cowley saw it and despite Stadden's coughed remarks about sentimentality knew Darby had come back to see his daughter. Find the girl, and they'd find Darby. Stadden said she lived in Lewisham.

'Who else knows?'

'Most of your suspects. The Banker certainly does. And the K.G.B., of course.'

'If he goes to her – he's dead.'

'I'd say so.' Stadden's hoarse voice remained deep. 'But give Darby his due – he's a pro. At least, he was. Maybe senility – and sentimentality – breed carelessness.'

To Cowley's way of thinking this tough old bird who took all this as he might an engrossing play represented a ghost from the past with teeth. Shrewdly, Cowley surmised that Thomas Darby would be just such another tough old ghost.

'Thank you, Brigadier.'

'Please.' Stadden waved a hand. 'I like to give you new boys all the help I can.' Cowley gave him a sour look and Doyle who had packed the projector took down the screen. 'It's just like old times,' said Stadden, with a satisfied sigh. 'With Darby hellbent on stirring it all up again.'

As Cowley and Doyle saw themselves out, Stadden called: 'Good hunting.' But as they left the good-humoured expression on his face changed to one of grim purpose. He rolled the wheel chair over to the phone table and dialled out to Sorenson.

As the phone rang, he said to himself with great bitterness: 'Just like old times . . .'

'Hallo?' He spoke harshly now. 'Is that you, Sorenson? This is Stadden – Yes, Stadden. I just thought you, and some of the others, might like to know. Thomas Darby is back. That's right. Probably here in London.'

In his basement bed-sitter in a not very salubrious part of London, Sorenson spoke into the phone to Stadden. He was a wreck of a man, grey, dull, with bitter eyes. His clothes were a sloppy mess and the bed-sitter stank. As he listened to Stadden the hate and anger grew in him, agonisingly, opening up old wounds.

'Oh, yes, I'll tell them.' He rubbed his leg, and winced at the old familiar hateful pain. 'Thank you, sir. Thank you.'

Sorenson put down the phone. His eyes looked for a moment as though he surveyed an old hell. Slowly and painfully he got to his feet and limped over to the chest of drawers. He took a cigar box from the bottom drawer. He moved with a slow deliberation. From the cigar box he took a 9mm Beretta M1951 Automatic. The pistol was well-kept, clean and with a film of clean oil. He hefted it in his hand. There were spare magazines, loaded, and a box of ammunition. He walked with a limp, and his movements were slow and stiff – but he slapped the mag into the pistol and pulled the slide back and cocked the gun – and these movements spoke eloquently of a man who knew all about small arms...

The manager of the small hotel in the Paddington area was absolutely fed up, stiff with rage – why did these gun-happy idiots have to choose his establishment? Bodie, who had gone to the hotel first, brought Cowley up to date. Cowley was still simmering over the information he had picked up from Stadden.

'We got this call from C.I. Central to say that Liam O'Leary came in. He was picked up at Heathrow from an Aer Lingus –'

'O'Leary,' said Cowley with disgust and contempt. 'The jackal of Dublin.'

'They said he was safely tabbed by their Duty Man at the airport, and followed. The Duty Man's name was Forrester, newly transferred from Military Intelligence. Pietro Callinari came in from Amsterdam about the same time.'

'Another Jackal.' Cowley looked at the sleazy room. 'Like dogs around a bone.'

'Anyway, Forrester on his own initiative decided to jump O'Leary. He had his driver as back-up.'

The police and C.I.D. men from local had gone. The ambulance men had removed the body. But on the floor thick chalk outlines indicated where the shot man had collapsed. The odd thing was – he'd fallen in the doorway so that now, with the door closed, only the upper half of his chalk-marked torso was visible. Cowley looked at that pathetic and gruesome outline.

'Didn't do him much good.'

'Forrester took two slugs in the chest as soon as he bust in the door. O'Leary took off out of the window. But at least he left his gear behind. Lewis got on to the scene early enough to get this.'

Bodie handed across a photograph. Cowley stared. The photograph showed the worn features of Tom Darby.

Cowley frowned. 'Target photo.' He looked up and spoke to Lewis who stood by the door. 'Anyone else see it?' At Lewis's shake of the head, Cowley puffed out his cheeks. 'Thank God for small mercies.' His little gesture indicated appreciation for Lewis's prompt action. Then: 'The Banker's bringing them in. He's the only one who could afford two of the most expensive hit-men in Europe.'

Abruptly, with a change of mood, Cowley lowered down on Bodie. 'So where's Callinari?'

'Lost. He gave the C.I. men the slip around Tottenham Court Road.'

'Damn!' Cowley glared down at the photograph of Darby. Anyone could get lost around T.C.R., that was true. But O'Leary and Callinari – call them thugs, call them hit-men, call them murderers, they were ugly customers. 'All this for Tom Darby.' He shook his head. 'It has to be more than just sentimentality.'

Bodie favoured his chief with a startled look, non-plussed by talk of sentimentality in this racket. But Bodie hadn't yet been briefed about the Stadden viewpoint. A knock sounded on the door and Lewis checked, and then opened to admit Doyle.

'We've got Helen Pierce's address,' Doyle announced. 'Low rental area. Must be hard-up. I've got it watched – '

Cowley said: 'She there?'

'No.'

'I want you two watching the place.' Cowley made his mind up fast; but Bodie and Doyle exchanged sour looks. 'I want to know when Helen Pierce gets back. The *moment* she gets back. I want to know the instant Darby shows. Or O'Leary. Or Callinari. Or Yashinkov's heavies.'

Bodie, in a low aside said: 'Or Uncle Tom Cobley . . . '

Cowley snarled at him. 'Or anyone! You said something about dust. Well, that's right. Twenty-year-old dust – but it's lethal! It can still choke you to death.' He pointed at the chalk outline. 'Ask him!'

With that, George Cowley started for the door. Doyle looked at the chalk outline so gruesomely cut by the closed door.

'Was it Forrester?'

Bodie said: 'Yes.'

'I knew him.'

Cowley turned back. 'Then you knew a bloody fool!'

And, on that, he stalked out.

Chapter Eight

Thomas Darby walked slowly in through the gate of the cemetery. The taxi that had brought him here from the train terminus departed, with the taxi-driver's last words still hanging in Darby's mind.

'Not a very cheerful place to drop you, guv. Still, we've all got to go sometime.'

The cemetery looked like an iced cake that had been turned over in a K.G.B. raid. The monuments glimmered in the pale sunshine, lichened, grey or brown, a few stark white stones reminding that the work of Death went on every day. Darby moved slowly along the gravel path. The place was very quiet, and the shadows under the trees looked colder than they should on a sunny day.

He was close to seventy now – a ridiculous age for a man who had done the things he had done – and he moved with a caution that, to those few people who knew him, came not from age but from his profession. He wore a suit rather too baggy, rather too out of date, a worn suit. He had discarded the spectacles he still did not need after he'd disembarked from the ferry at Dover. The train journey through the fields of England had awoken painful and nostalgic memories. But he had been dedicated to the Party all his life. He had made his decisions in the light of his beliefs. Spain, now, had not been able to shake those. And there was Eileen, too – he walked on towards the grave he had come to see.

He looked just a tired old man. A trained observer would have noticed that little something that set him apart from the ordinary run of men. But that made no difference. He was a tired old man and he had come home to die.

And, as well, as the fellows would have said at University so long ago – come home to die, *inter alia.*

Darby saw the woman dressed all in black just rising from one of the newer headstones. She was in her mid-twenties, and she looked slender and somehow isolated in the desolation of death. He saw her face. He felt his tired old heart go *thump.* He knew who she was. Knew at once.

He walked carefully up to her and she was engrossed in her task of tidying up the flowers on the grave. He looked down. The stone was simple. It was brand new and in it, in simple Roman lettering, were carved a few words.

EILEEN PIERCE. 1912–1978 R.I.P.

In a hushed voice, Darby said: 'Hello, Helen.'

She swung about, startled, a limp flower falling from her fingers. She frowned at him, seeing no immediate menace in this old fellow, the well-brushed shabby coat.

'I'm sorry – I . . . Do I know you?'

Suddenly, like clouds over still water, a host of emotions passed over her pale features. Darby saw shock there, and incredulity and disbelief. Did he see fear? She opened her mouth and tried to speak, and swallowed. She swayed. Her eyes closed. Then she had recovered herself. She stared at him.

'You . . .'

Helen saw the square, saggy face, the lines soft and the skin somehow falling away, so that his face looked like a badly-stuffed pillow. The colour was not right, either, far too yellow. But his eyes held a warm friendly look, and he smiled.

'The prodigal father.'

Helen could not stop the sob. She tried to turn to her father and hold him – but he restrained her, putting his hand firmly on her arm, keeping her away.

'Keep looking at your mother's grave. Please – please try to act normally. I'm sorry if I gave you a shock.'

She put a hand to her face, her fingers trembled.

'Normally . . .'

'There was no easy way of contacting you. And I could give you no warning, my dear.'

'You appear from nowhere after twenty years and say "act normally"?' She looked hard at him, seeing what time had done to him – time and experience. 'Do the authorities know you're back? How did you get here?'

'Old tricks and good luck. They probably know.'

'You are in danger!'

'It really doesn't matter –'

'Yes, it does!'

'No. I'm all right.' He did not look all right. He looked as though the first sneeze would blow him right over. He was in the right place for that. 'I still have an instinct for all this. I can still make myself invisible. It's a knack.'

Helen whispered, reading years of loneliness into the words. She swayed against him. 'Oh, father . . .'

'An old talent,' said Darby, and the tired muffling of his voice only partially obliterated the bitterness.

Presently they walked along the gravel paths. A funeral entered the gates, the limousines imposing and distant, the heaped flowers on their roofs patched with colour. Darby was saying: 'It would be quite understandable if you despised me.'

'How can I despise you? I don't understand what you did – or why you did it – but I couldn't hate you for it.'

'Then the rest doesn't matter.' He turned to look a last time at the tombstone. 'Perhaps she understood.'

'My mother loved you until the day she died.'

'She wasn't in pain – or –'

'No.'

'Thank God for that. Did she ever speak to you of a

solicitor? Someone who looked after her affairs?'

'Yes –'

'It's the same man?'

Darby's voice betrayed nothing of any other emotions than the obvious ones. He could feel the pain inside him gnawing away and, as always, he ignored it.

Helen said: 'Yes, I suppose so. There wasn't much for him ever to do. But he's looked after things for –'

'– over twenty years. Good.'

The pain caught Darby then, and he winced and stuck his fist into his side, under the heart. Helen gasped.

'You're not well! Are you?'

His smile trembled for her. 'No. I'm afraid not.'

A sense of exhausting weight hung about Darby. The trees, the headstones, the church, the oncoming funeral, all added to that sense of suffocation. Helen took his arm, looking with concern into his face.

Limping slowly and painfully up past the newly-turned graves beyond the end of a line of trees, Sorenson saw his quarry with a woman. He pressed on as fast as he could. The expression on Sorenson's face would have frightened a camp guard. Elsa had acted as he had expected the moment he'd told her Darby was back, and her little car was a God-send. But this was something he had to do – for himself, for Elsa, for all of them.

He took the Beretta out of his pocket and limped on as quickly as he could. The black hearse passed along the gravel path ahead of him, obscuring Darby and the woman. The limousines followed, crunching slowly, the flowers brilliant on their roofs, the silhouettes of the mourners within like waxworks. Sorenson puffed along up the slope.

When the funeral procession had passed he looked up – there was no sign of Thomas Darby. The man had vanished – again.

The little street of terraced houses here in South London had once been respectable. Each house was the same, with its tiny bay-fronted downstairs window to the front room, two foot of garden, a door with tiny glass panels – once the doors were all flogged with beer into marvels of artificial wood-grainings. The houses had been around fifteen bob a week rent, and the lace curtains were clean and white, the aspidistras green and shiny. Now the front doors were painted in modern garish colours, the gardens were junk heaps with dustbins, half the houses were bed-sits and many were boarded up. The neighbourhood was run down. A few cars rusted gently at the kerb. Among them Bodie's car – he'd not taken the Capri on a job like this – sat waiting. The car was a six-year-old Vauxhall. Bodie sat at the wheel and Doyle slouched back in the front passenger seat, and they kept an obbo on Helen Pierce's house over the way.

Doyle yawned. 'I wonder just how good they were?'

'Who?'

'The old brigade. The spies who came in from the cold. Brigadier Stadden's mob.'

Bodie's mobile lips drew up in a half-smile. 'All dark corners, back alleys – and grey dust.'

'Cowley thinks they were good. He was just starting in then.'

Bodie said, quoting Cowley: 'Never send a boy on a man's errand. They'll pinch his bike.' He smile slipped. 'George Cowley. Words of Wisdom. Chapter One. He came in just after Darby went missing. Darby pinched the bike.'

All the time they talked they kept their eyes open. Lewis was around the back in the little twitten that ran between the houses. Doyle, as the ex-detective-constable, was used to this kind of job, keeping an observation was a boring part of the routine. For the colourful Bodie, ex-para, ex-mercenary, ex just about everything lurid, the waiting frayed at his nerves.

'Cowley knows general surveillance drives me right up the wall . . .'

'Relax,' said Doyle, amused.

'Lift my mind on to a higher transcendental plane?'

'Yeah. Like – what won the 2.30 at Haydock Park?'

Bodie had to smile; he was supposed to be the betting man.

Then Doyle sat up. 'I've just had a nasty thought!'

'You forgot,' Bodie surmised. 'To ring your bookie.'

'Better check inside.'

Bodie nodded towards Helen's house. 'She's not there. Lewis said – '

'She may not be there. Doesn't mean to say she hasn't got visitors waiting, though. O'Leary and Callinari are pros. They're not going to walk up to the place in broad daylight. One of us'll have to take a look.' He produced a florin. 'Call.'

'Heads.'

In some disgust Doyle looked at the tenpenny piece on his palm. 'Two bleeps if anyone shows, O.K.?' Doyle put the coin back in his pocket, produced a set of skeleton keys, and then opened the car door. He stared back at Bodie. 'And for God's sake – stay alert, hey?'

Taking it nice and easy Doyle ambled up the street a way and then cut across the road and ducked down the side alley to come up behind the house. He checked with Lewis and then tried the back gate. It was locked. Well, that was a relief. The skeleton key opened the gate and he went quickly up the cracked concrete path to the back door and, opening that with another key, let himself in. The house brooded in silence, smelling of polish and turpentine and not a trace of cabbage.

Despite the sun shining outside, the little house was dark. Doyle went carefully along the passage. The stairs led away up to his right and the front room door showed to his left. A hallstand contained a few outdoor things. The carpet was thin. But the place was highly polished. The door to the living-room to his left, set back from the front room, opened slowly to reveal an even deeper darkness. Doyle peeked in.

Then – he was an ex-copper. He was a Professional, working for C.I.5, the Big A, the Squad. Ray Doyle *knew* someone was standing behind that half-open door. Someone who breathed lightly. Someone waiting with deadly intent...

Doyle drew his Browning auto silently.

He gave the door a savage thrust inwards.

The door belted back and slammed into a big, swarthy man with a thin black moustache. He yelped and staggered. That was all Doyle saw as he crashed through and followed up with a thundering slash from his free left hand. The man was Callinari. No mistake.

Callinari yelled.

Doyle whipped up the Browning auto, covering the big hit-man.

He sensed the movement at his back before he heard anything. He knew just who it was back there, he knew what was going to happen, and he tried desperately to dodge away.

But O'Leary's gun barrel sledged down on Doyle's bare head.

Ray Doyle went over in a heap, his automatic flying from nerveless fingers.

O'Leary stepped through.

Callinari's savage words in quick Sicilian slang meant nothing beside his actions. He ripped out his own gun and pointed it at Doyle's head. The big man's face twisted with hatred. His finger tightened on the trigger.

With a contemptuous gesture, O'Leary pushed the gun away and bent to Doyle. He riffled through the C.I.5 man's jacket and came up with the walkie-talkie.

The two professional assassins looked at the prone form of the professional C.I.5 agent. Ray Doyle lay there, out to the world, unknowing how close death hovered.

George Cowley's itchy nose took him once again to see Brigadier Stadden. The old man sat in his wheelchair, a plaid rug over his knees, and his big beaked face peered up gauntly like the head of an eagle. They sat in the study and ran through what they had, and, all the time, in

Cowley's mind the thought: this man sitting shrunken before him could be the Banker.

Stadden said, with his sniff and indrawn breath: 'So he's come home to die. Prompted by the death of his mistress – and a need to see his forgotten love child.'

Tautly, pressing, Cowley said: 'It's more than that.'

Idly, plucking at his blanket, Stadden said: 'To taste a pint of bitter again. See an oak tree in leaf. Walk a country lane –'

Cowley was not deceived. 'More,' he insisted.

'Does it matter?'

You could see Stadden's point of view, Cowley thought; old, tired, crippled, reliving ancient memories. You got like that in the end, and all that mattered was creature comfort. But there was a man at large who should be brought to book for his activities – even Stadden had to recognise that.

'Yes!' said Cowley, fiercely.

Stadden sighed. 'You may be right.'

'I know damn well I'm right!'

From under the plaid blanket Stadden drew out a book. It was a hardcover book, thick, large, and its jacket of bright colours and hard-hitting blurbs was tattered but still shiny.

'I expect,' said Stadden in his grape-chewing way. 'You've read this?'

'Thomas Darby's book –'

'*Red Spy at Night.*'

'Yes, I've read it.'

'Most people have. It was on the bestseller list.'

Stadden leafed through the book. He spoke in a contemptuous way, in an almost valedictory way, and he touched the pages as though the feel of the book disgusted him.

'It doesn't,' Cowley pointed out patiently, 'tell us anything we don't already know.'

'That's right.' Stadden closed the book. He swallowed and his Adam's apple jumped. He spoke as though his mouth was full of spittle. 'Supposed to be a big exposé – but it turned out to be a damp squib. Some say it was written by a bunch of *Pravda* journalists. Still – it sold a few million. It should have made Darby a rich man. But it didn't.' He plucked at the blanket over his knees. 'Royalties – those they bothered to collect – would all go to the State.'

Cowley listened carefully. He waited, and then said: 'So?'

'Enough to turn a man sour.'

'Still not reason enough.' Cowley shook his head. 'The book's written. That's history.'

Stadden's thick voice expressed a distant amusement. He was in a sloth-like way enjoying this. 'It's not the book he *could* have written. Probably *did* write.' He looked at Cowley. 'Yes. His own records, his diaries, his *own* story – the truth.' He was still looking at Cowley with those old eagle eyes over the beaked nose. 'The whole chronicle. Naming real names, real places, real proof – blowing every facet of the Establishment sky high. That's what *Red Spy at Night should* have been.'

'A second book somewhere.' Cowley stood up and moved a few paces away and then came back. 'Naming real names – like that of the Banker.'

'Be worth a fortune.'

'He'd never get it published – not here. But foreign publishers would jump at it. Dynamite. They'd pay anything for it –'

'Anything,' Stadden said in his choked way, 'he'd care to ask.'

Cowley saw it now. 'Enough to keep Helen Pierce in comfort for the rest of her life . . .'

Stadden looked lost, now, hunched down in his wheelchair.

Pacing back, Cowley blazed up. 'Yes, that'd bring Darby back. A bequest to his daughter. Sell it to a foreign publisher, deed the royalties to her – and then die in peace.'

'And blow up another hundred people.' The quietness of the choked words could not conceal the old bitterness.

'A second manuscript . . .' said Cowley, thinking.

'Stirring it up again.' Stadden was talking to himself now, oblivious of Cowley's presence. 'Stirring it, even from his grave.'

'His mistress.' Cowley nodded. 'Eileen Pierce. She'd be the only one he could trust it with –'

That got through to Stadden. He looked up, plucking at the plaid over his knees, and his eyes were bright with malicious humour. 'And she's dead.'

The two professional hit men dragged Doyle into the front room and threw his limp body down on the carpet. His mouth was sealed with tape, and his hands were knotted up into the small of his back. He was still out cold. They put his pistol and radio intercom on the table in the centre of the room, beside the bowl of flowers. They sprawled out in the two armchairs, one each side of the cold gas fire. There were three ducks in flight along the wall, and the sideboard was cluttered with photographs. Presently Callinari got up and went to the curtained window and peeked out.

'No need to watch, Cal.' O'Leary pointed to the walkie-talkie. 'That'll tell us when anyone gets worried.'

'How do we get out?'

'Don't worry.'

Callinari shook his head. He was a big man, with a swarthy skin and a blue jaw; but he looked worried. 'Too many close shaves –'

'I had a close shave, me lad. And, for the money we're getting – I'll take on anything they throw at me.'

Callinari wasn't happy. 'Maybe he hasn't contacted her yet. Maybe she don't know anything –'

'We'll see.' O'Leary suddenly revealed the viciousness underlying all his words and actions. He was a Jackal of the worst stripe, gutter-violence was his trade-in-hand. His eyes repelled by their fish-like coldness, the flatness of their stare. 'We'll get something out of her.'

The bleeper call squirted two sharp bleeps into the room. Both men swung to stare at the intercom.

Together, they crossed to the window and with the skill

of long experience looked out. No one out there would spot them. With a nod, O'Leary, taking a hard look at the bound form of Doyle, left the window and went out into the hall. He took his pistol out and gave it a quick, unthinking check.

The sound of quick footfalls on the little path and then the scrape of the Yale key in the lock brought O'Leary up, ready.

The door opened. As Helen entered she was for a moment or two disorientated by the gloom of the house after the sunshine in the street. In those few heartbeats O'Leary pounced.

His hard hand raked around her face and his fingers clamped on her jaws cruelly. The gun barrel jammed in under her ear where the hair curled. He pushed hard, hurting the girl.

'One squeak,' he said in that menacing tone of voice he had no need to invent. 'One twitch . . . !'

Absolutely terrified, shocked, Helen attempted to struggle. Her movements were those of a chicken caught in the jaws of a fox. O'Leary tightened his grip sadistically, and Helen flopped limply, unable to gasp, the fingers digging into her mouth. She subsided.

Callinari appeared in the front room doorway.

'Get back to that window!' snarled O'Leary. 'And watch!'

Callinari disappeared promptly. Only an idiot hell-bent on suicide argued with O'Leary when he had the fey look in his eyes.

Slowly, the gunman eased the pressure on Helen. He took his hand from her mouth and the marks of fingers stood out whitely, corpse marks on her soft skin. He showed her the gun.

'D'you know something, Helen Pierce? There are a couple've dozen places in the human body where a ballet can hurt and maim – but not kill. Pain like you've never dreamed. I know 'em all.'

She swayed. Her emotions had taken a battering this

morning and now – now this! 'What,' she gasped, shaking. 'What do you want?'

'Oh, now, you know what I want, Helen. Just two scraps of information.'

'I don't know what you –'

'And I've no time for messing. No time at all. I want to know where your father is at this moment.'

Helen shook her head. Her face was bloodless. She could feel all the blood pounding in her head, hurting her, and it was difficult to breathe . . .

'And I want to know where his papers are hidden. They're not here – we've turned over the place.' He gripped her arm and the grip branded her like white-hot iron. 'But they're around somewhere.'

He pushed the gun into her stomach, making her gasp. There was no chance she would act like a professional in these circumstances. The feel of the gun made O'Leary conscious of his own power. The girl would talk, and, faith, she'd talk quick! 'Now, first off – where is Thomas Darby?'

Helen was gasping, struggling to draw breath, her head aching and hurting, her stomach contracting from the hard steel gun muzzle. 'I can't . . . I can't . . .'

'You can – and you will.'

O'Leary lifted the gun again and pointed it between her eyes.

'Why can't you leave him alone?' Helen cried. 'He's just an old man . . . He's ill . . . He just wants . . .'

O'Leary started to pull the trigger – gently.

'Where?'

Now the tears of terror streamed freely down Helen's cheeks. She shivered. She was breaking and couldn't stop herself. This kind of ghastly nightmare was completely outside her experience. She shook and spoke frenziedly.

'Oh God . . . He's round the back somewhere . . . He's waiting for me to signal him . . .'

O'Leary let rip a shout of triumph.

'You hear that, Callinari!'

'Yes.' Callinari's voice rasped from the front room, impatiently. 'Hurry it up, will you? I want to know how we get out of here.'

O'Leary gave Helen's arm a wholly unnecessary twist, making her gasp anew. She sagged, like a little child too tired to walk upstairs to bed. 'Does he have the manuscript with him?'

'I don't know about any manuscript . . .' The tears were choking her. Her head hurt. Her stomach seemed on fire where this beast had jammed his gun. 'Honest to God, I don't.'

In the front room Callinari beat his free left hand in a soft irritated tattoo against the window frame. Nothing was going on outside. He listened to O'Leary questioning the girl and although he didn't give a damn what happened to her he could feel it in his heart to shudder at the fate of anyone who crossed O'Leary. He turned half-back from the window, moving to pass around the table, determined to get this thing over with.

On the floor two bright blue eyes peered up from the shadows over Doyle's face. He felt lousy; but he had heard enough to know what was going on. The table stood at his feet and Callinari was beyond. Doyle doubled up. Then, with tremendous force he shot his legs out and shoved the table like a ramrod. The table slammed into Callinari's midriff. The assassin threw his arms up and went backwards. He went clean through the window. The glass shattered, the frame split, the curtains ripped. Out he went like a cannon-ball. His pistol let rip into the ceiling, bringing down plaster. The noise boomed like the Battle of Trafalgar. He went out through the front window smothered in glass fragments, trailing splintered wood and tangling curtains. He hit in the scrap of garden and he did not get up.

When Callinari catapulted through the window creating the most infernal din of shattering glass and pistol shots, Bodie was over half-way across the road to Helen's house. He had decided he couldn't hang about any longer waiting for Doyle. Now he drew his gun and ran up to the front door and slammed his foot against the lock without making any attempt to try the door. The door shot back shedding splinters of yellow wood. Bodie flattened to the side, waited – silence – crouched over he sprang into the hall and pressed against the wallpaper.

Shadows and smells of polish intermingled with gun-smoke – and silence. He crouched and looked down the hall as a slight noise reached him. He took aim and the rear door opened and it was Lewis, coming in cróuched, ready to shoot.

'Cover the back!' yelled Bodie and jumped up. A muffled drumming sound came from the front room. Taking due precautions, Bodie entered the room ready to blast the guts from anybody taking a pot-shot at him. He saw Doyle, bound and gagged, banging his heels on the floor.

Without ceremony Bodie ripped the tape from Doyle's mouth. His knife appeared in his hand as though he was an Apache and a single slash severed Doyle's bonds.

The returning blood made Doyle jump about, but he gasped out: 'O'Leary's in here somewhere. He's got the girl. And Darby's out the back!'

Shaking himself like a dog paddling ashore from the sea, Doyle grabbed his own gun from where it had been thrown when the table did its dirty work. 'What about the Italian?'

Bodie smiled nastily. 'Out of it for the moment.'

Together they made for the front-room door and came out cautiously into the hall. Half-way up the stairs Helen stood, shrinking back, her face frightened, tear-streaked, her hair a mess. O'Leary stood behind her, one arm around her waist and constricting her in. His right hand held his gun shoved up under the girl's ear.

The gunman did not seem in the slightest perturbed by the events of the past few moments. He smiled his leering smile, looking down over Helen's drooping shoulder at the two C.I.5 men.

'Easy, lads. Easy. You know I've nothin' to lose.'

Carefully, Bodie and Doyle backed off.

Bodie spoke contemptuously. 'You'll get about a hundred yards. You're in the middle of London.'

'About a hundred yards, y'say?' He pushed Helen down to the next step. All the bright vicious confidence in him sickened the two below. 'Well, we'll have to see now, won't we?'

Speaking in his gruff policeman's voice, Doyle said: 'It's all over, chum.'

'Not by a long chalk it isn't!' Another step down, with the gun muzzle pressing against Helen's head. 'Keep your distance – or I'll blow her head off!'

He edged down and pushed Helen across the thin carpet to the front door which gaped open where Bodie's kick had shattered it. With a quick, bird-like look out, O'Leary turned and backed out, still gripping Helen, still holding the gun. He dragged the girl with him now. His face showed all the marks of bright and sadistic triumph. The girl's life hung dizzily, worth nothing if Bodie and Doyle made a single false move.

O'Leary backed away down the path.

Doyle turned and, cupping his mouth, bellowed into the back area of the house.

'Lewis!'

The answer came from Lewis unseen out by the back.

'Yeah?'

'Darby's out the back somewhere. Find him!'

'O.K.'

Bodie and Doyle, their Brownings ready – and quite useless – moved out of the front door.

The quiet run-down street showed signs of neighbourhood activity. Doyle wasn't prepared to call it neighbourly activity. A few people shoved their heads out of the bedroom windows upstairs, and a few stood half in their fractionally-opened doorways. The excitement buzzed in the air as the gunman, dragging Helen, backed off along the street. A car pulled out from a dozen or so houses along and straightened up.

Bodie and Doyle reached the pavement, wary of the gunman, ready to take him the moment the break came. The car roared up at their backs. Deliberately, the car mounted the pavement.

With a rushing roar it swooped at the two C.I.5 men.

With startled yells, Doyle and Bodie threw themselves back out of the way of the car. It slashed past, the tyres jouncing over the kerb, hit the road again, slewed, straightened up and skidded to a partial halt beside O'Leary. The rear passenger door opened and O'Leary hurled Helen in. The car was moving off with spinning tyres as he bundled in after. The door slammed, the car smoked away.

Instantly Bodie was up and racing for the old Vauxhall. Doyle followed and they leaped into the car, started up, ready to hurtle off in chase.

Thomas Darby, quiet, inconspicuous, stood in the shadows of the twitten running between the backs of the houses. He was watching the big man who was watching the house. There had been gunfire and crashes and the sounds of strife. Darby waited until the man was looking up the other way and quickly dodged across the twitten to the mouth of the alley leading on to the street.

There were two ways to go in the twitten and only one of Lewis . . . He just didn't see Darby slip out.

Darby hurried to the corner, knowing something had gone wrong, anxious, feeling the pain in him – he rounded the alley corner and almost collided with the man holding the blue-gleaming Beretta. The automatic jabbed into his stomach. He stopped, panting only a little, and tiredly looked up.

Sorenson said: 'Hello, Tom.'

He spoke quietly; but the venom of years of pain jagged under the words. Darby looked, glanced down at the pistol, and his shoulders sagged.

'Sorenson . . .'

'Nice,' said Sorenson, tired and old and filled with pain, half-sneering now, 'Nice of you to remember.' He tapped his bad leg. It was drilling a pain into him now like a maniac dentist on the loose. 'I think of you, too. Every time there's a bloody chill in the air.'

He gestured with the Beretta. An old Mini stood at the kerb, quite unremarkable in that street of rusting wrecks.

'You know the routine,' said Sorenson. 'Get in.'

They got in and the Mini moved off just as Lewis came belting out of the alley. Frustration showed on the C.I.5 man's face. But he saw the car's number and he ripped a notebook free and jotted it down before he grabbed for his walkie-talkie.

The old Mini trundled away in the opposite direction to that in which Bodie's Vauxhall was picking up speed in pursuit of O'Leary and Helen Pierce. The Vauxhall tore down the centre of the road between the lines of cars.

'Just keep on his tail,' shouted Doyle. He grabbed his walkie-talkie.

'Yeh, well – use that thing! Get us some muscle.' Bodie looked ahead and his mouth curved into a sour line. 'Cowley's just going to love this!'

Staring ahead Bodie saw the big black limousine pull out from the line of parked cars. The limousine was quite out of place here in the normal way – a car like that would be seen here for weddings and funerals. It hauled out across the road and Bodie started to curse and rave. O'Leary's car went hurtling on up the road beyond the limousine. Doyle looked up and saw and instinctively threw his hands up to protect his face from the seemingly inevitable collision.

With a tyre-screaming skid the Vauxhall slewed as Bodie hauled savagely on the wheel. His foot smashed down on to the brake. The Vauxhall shuddered like a horse under the lash. It quivered and slewed, hit the kerb, bounced up, came to a jouncing stop mere inches from the limousine.

Furious, Bodie and Doyle leaped from their car and raced to the limousine. They yanked the doors open and hauled out two men, big, burly men with square, doughy faces, dressed in solid un-English clothes.

Doyle shoved an arm lock on his man, and the fellow just smiled. 'Up the workers, tovarich,' he said, smirking.

Bodie's fist was cocked to slam a destructive punch full in his man's kisser. But he checked as he recognised the man.

'Are-essenal for the Cup?'

Bodie glared. The bloody Ivans had done it again! Bodie's look was compounded of a world-weary knowledge and the frustration at what had happened. All he could say stupidly, was: 'Da.'

Chapter Nine

'Beautiful!' said George Cowley. He was in an icy rage. He swung back from the shattered window where Callinari had backed off into destruction from that battering-ram table of Doyle's. 'Beautiful, isn't it? The whole operation turned from a viable proposition into an utter shambles inside the space of a few hours. What sort of story d'you think I'm going to concoct for the police? How do I keep this out of the damn papers, eh?'

'I thought,' offered Bodie, 'a full clamp-down –'

Cowley thundered on regardless. '*Thought!* What bloody thought? You've never had a decent thought between the pair of you. Half the street saw Helen Pierce dragged away!'

An ambulance siren wailed away and the blue flashing light of one of the police cars in the street flickered erratically through the gaping window.

'We've got Callinari,' said Doyle, rather more defensively than he relished. 'If we can get the shrinks on to him we can get something out of him –'

'When he went through that window,' said Cowley in his most cutting way, 'the glass made a fair job on his throat. He won't be doing any talking for months – *if* he lives.'

The three glared at one another, feeling the pressures clamping down, frustration and anger simmering beneath everything they said and did. Finally Bodie, being Bodie, had to say it.

'If it hadn't been for Yashinkov's hatchet men . . . I mean, we didn't expect them . . . '

'Then you should have done!' Cowley gestured, a sharp, irritated chop of his right hand. 'Yashinkov *had* to protect the Banker. For all we know, Yashinkov probably set up the whole thing. Of course he would be somewhere on the side-lines. Had to be.'

'We could have tailed O'Leary,' said Doyle, stubbornly.

'And then what? He's not about to blaze a trail for us. Or did you expect him to lead you by the right hand up to the Banker's front door? And what about Darby? Where the devil is he now?' Cowley fairly snarled it out. 'And his manuscript? A shambles. A complete and utter shambles.'

'Well,' said Doyle, after a tiny pause to let the chief get his wind back. 'We're not the only ones who have lost Darby, sir. O'Leary's lost him too.'

Bodie pounced on that, trying to take the heat off.

'The only thing he can do now is go after the manuscript.'

The Mini drove steadily and carefully so as not to attract the slightest unwelcome attention. In the back Sorenson sat, stiffly, the Beretta covering Darby. The temptation to pull the trigger had passed; now Sorenson would go on with the plan.

'Where are you taking me? Somewhere to kill me?'

'Are you under the impression you don't deserve a bullet, Darby?'

Slowly, yet with the old dedication still there, Darby said: 'I was just doing my job. Like you. I took up the Cause when I was nineteen. I've been a serving officer of the K.G.B. all my adult life – '

'But you carry no wounds?' Sorenson spoke thickly. He jerked his head at the driver. 'Do you recognise our driver?

No – I don't suppose so. She looked very different when you were her Controller. She had long blonde hair. Slim. Lovely.' As Sorenson spoke, Darby looked at the straggly grey hair of the woman driving, saw the way she slumped in the seat, the gnarled hands on the wheel. 'But she aches now,' Sorenson said, his voice thick and ugly and yet resigned, as though awaiting somebody else to pull the trigger. 'Just like me.'

'Who is it?'

'Just another name. Just another victim. They picked her up in East Germany. She was at a safe house. She and two others when they came for her. A house you had organised.'

Darby shivered. 'Oh God – Elsa. Elsa Coran.'

'That's right.' The Mini rounded a corner and the familiar London streets passed with the red buses and the taxis and traffic, the people in bright summer clothes walking on the pavement, the air of bustle all about – but these three were locked in memories of another time and another place – another world . . . 'The other two were executed – in camera. She was two years in the Interrogation Camp. She never speaks of what they did to her.' Sorenson grunted as the pain hit him, triggered by these dark memories. 'We're an exclusive little club, Darby, those of us who survived. We always think of you as our – Founder.'

Thomas Darby sat, shrunken, thoughts and memories jostling his tired brain. Sorenson – and Elsa Coran – yes, and all the others killed or maimed because he had done what he conceived of as his duty. He did not have much longer to live, he was calmly assured of that. Perhaps, in the end, none of it mattered, didn't matter a damn . . .

Lewis replaced the handset of the police car's radio, nodded thanks to the driver, and went back into Helen Pierce's house. 'Elsa Coran, sir,' he said. 'And Martin Sorenson – retired Civil Servant – '

'Grey, mousy little man?' interrupted Cowley.

Lewis said: 'Yes – ' Bodie said: 'You know him sir?'

'Yes, I know him.' Cowley spoke quietly, evenly. 'More of your dust, Bodie. Martin Sorenson is an ex-S.I.S. man. One of Brigadier Stadden's old mob. One of the many agents Tom Darby put the finger on when he defected. The K.G.B. rounded him up – gave him hell. We exchanged him at the Berlin Wall fifteen years ago. He was in hospital for eighteen months afterwards.' The house was empty now save for the C.I.5 people, and the place seemed to echo Cowley's words. 'You can imagine how he feels about Thomas Darby.'

'And Elsa Coran?' Doyle felt the sombreness of these old events, dust stirring from the past – with death as the final payoff.

'The same story. We might never hear of Darby again. Never. Sorenson could bury him deeper than a coal mine. Not even Yashinkov and an army of Ivans – or O'Leary and a battalion of hit-men – would ever find him.' He scowled at the implications. 'And that would be awkward.'

'Sorenson and Elsa Coran,' said Doyle. 'They're survivors – so – execution?'

'Well, Sorenson's not going to play tiddle-winks with him, is he? So, for the moment, let's concentrate on finding O'Leary and Helen Pierce.'

Together, Bodie and Doyle said: 'The lawyer.'

'Right. Arthur Pulford, solicitor. He's the only other connection between Darby and Helen's dead mother.' The C.I.5 men moved to the door and down the path, leaving that sad little house. Cowley reminded himself to get the boys out to patch up the smashed window. He went on: 'They were both clients of Pulford's, so it's logical to assume Pulford is still handling Eileen Pierce's estate.'

They went to Cowley's white Rover and Lewis took the Vauxhall. Cowley said as they started up: 'It is possible he would have all her papers and documents, including anything Darby left with her for safe keeping. The daughter probably knows all about Pulford. Sooner or later O'Leary will get his name and address out of her.' Cowley's face looked grim and forbidding. 'And if I know that Jackal O'Leary, it will be sooner rather than later.'

'Yeah, he's a nasty piece of work,' said Doyle.

Arthur Pulford's office was compounded of browns and ochres and dark greens, of the incense of the law, the dust of ages and bygone cases, of red ribbons and stiff parchment. The smell took one back to institutional schools, dust and polish and a scrubbed cleanness that never showed for long. The outer office contained the typewriter and the desk and the bound and gagged form of Pulford's secretary, terrified in her swivel chair, her eyes enormous, her shoulders quivering in the twin set.

The glass door to the inner office stood open. Along one wall the windows grudgingly let in some sunlight. The opposite wall was lined with deed boxes, each one locked and strapped up, marked with brown paper labels. Three people were in the room – Helen Pierce squatting terrified in a corner, unable to take her eyes off O'Leary who rummaged like a madman among the deed boxes. The third person was Arthur Pulford. He lay sprawled on his threadbare carpet, arms spread wide, a trickle of blood from his mouth and a black and red hole in his head.

In that stuffy legal office the stink of burnt gun powder battled against all the fusty smells of the dead years.

Some of the deed boxes fell over with a clatter on to the floor beyond the carpet. The olive-green metal of the newest ones was a relic of the late war. O'Leary hauled another out, looked at the label – and smiled. He hefted the box over on to Pulford's desk and then crossed to the glass door and closed it on the outer office and the bound secretary.

'Are you a betting lady, Helen?'

She was unable to speak. Like a rabbit before a snake, she just stared, shrivelled.

'I like a wager, if the odds are right.' O'Leary had come a long way from his native Dublin. He had shot and clubbed and stabbed his way through life, and had put the boot in for good measure. He just didn't bother to remember how many poor slobs he'd kneecapped on orders. He was murder for hire, he was good, he knew he was good – and he was half off his head most of the time. 'I'm betting there's a fortune in that box. Not in currency, you understand – but it's something that's worth the divil a lot to someone.'

He carried Pulford's cushion from the creaky mahogany rail-backed swivel chair over to the deed box, put it against the lock. He aimed his pistol carefully and through the cushion blew the lock away. The report was muffled; but the stink of fired powder thickened in the room.

Helen jerked uncontrollably as the gun went off.

A jumble of papers was thrown casually aside as O'Leary rifled through the box. He came up with a sealed manilla envelope. He smiled, the lean lines of his jaw tightening.

'Ah, bless your dear dead mother, Helen. She's not let us down.' He broke the red sealing wax, ripped the end off the envelope and drew out a thick bundle of manuscript. He put it down on the desk and then reached for Pulford's telephone and began to dial out. 'It's a great gift,' he said as the phone dial whirred. 'Being able to write. Indeed it is.'

The apparent naïvety of this remark, that of a schoolboy faced with writing an essay, choked Helen with horror. The idle thought occurred to her that O'Leary was dyslexic – but he could dial out a telephone number. He started to speak into the mouthpiece. His eyes switched from the manuscript, to Helen, to the glass door to the outer office. He did not bother to look at Arthur Pulford. When O'Leary shot a man, the man stayed shot.

Everything was working out fine for him. When he'd finished receiving his instructions, he knew he would have to kill the secretary out there, and kill Helen Pierce, too.

Well, that was what he was paid for, all part of the job. That he enjoyed his work was an added bonus . . .

When Cowley and Lewis walked up the stairs to the rear, Bodie and Doyle, who had run up like whirlwinds, flattened themselves out, one each side of the door. They drew their Brownings, and then looked at each other.

'Maybe he hasn't arrived yet,' suggested Doyle.

'That,' Bodie reminded his partner, 'is what we said last time.'

'It's going to be tight in there.'

'Like a spinster's girdle.'

Doyle leaned over and tried the doorknob. 'Yeah,' he said. 'Well . . . ' The knob turned easily and the door yielded. Doyle ducked back against the wall, gun up. Nothing happened. Slowly, he peered around the edge of the door, into the terrified eyes of a woman in a twin set and bonds, sitting gagged in a typist's chair. He looked, and slid in, low, shaking his head at her to keep quiet. Her eyes rolled like marbles, alerting him to the closed inner glass door.

Inside the office Doyle hesitated – he could call Bodie up or he could go on alone . . . He thought of Forrester – he took a step forward . . .

A floorboard in the old sagging floor creaked under his probing foot.

Two things happened at once.

Doyle hurled himself sideways and rolled against the wall.

The glass door smashed into a thousand fragments as a vicious burst of gunfire scythed through. The bullets gashed into the wall, shattering the glass in a picture of Arthur Pulford in fancy robes, and gouted a flower vase into spinning china chips.

The shadow of O'Leary appeared beyond the broken glass, pistol aimed, about to drive the last aimed shots into Doyle's prostrate body.

Bodie belted through the outer door, took it all in, saw that shadowed form with the upraised pistol, and triggered two quick shots from his Browning.

The slugs hit O'Leary in the chest, driving him back. He swivelled sideways, collapsing, clawing desperately and sending the sheets of manuscript billowing up into the room. Bodie roared in, ready to shoot again and keep on shooting for as long as was necessary. Doyle leaped up and followed him in. O'Leary tried to rise, tried to stand – but his legs buckled. He coughed bright red. He fell down and rolled, his arm flopped out limply, and he was dead.

Cowley and Lewis ran into the office – and only Lewis had his pistol drawn. Cowley's eyebrows drew down as he surveyed the carnage.

'See to the secretary, Lewis.' He glared at Bodie. 'O'Leary?'

Bodie indicated the bodies. 'They're both dead, sir.' He nodded at Helen. 'That's Helen Pierce – and she's pretty shaken.'

'You've a knack for stating the obvious, Bodie.' Cowley's voice had never been plummier. But he understood his men. Outsiders could not really be expected to understand why agents like Bodie and Doyle insisted on making terrible jokes all the time. Good Lord – how could you expect young men to witness scenes like this as part of the job the community called on them to perform, and remain sane without letting off something of the grotesqueness of it all? If corruption in the building industry was real life, then so was this murder and mayhem part of another real life. The lives of men and women depended on that manuscript not falling into the wrong hands. And, not only their lives, for – perhaps – death might be preferable to what Elsa Coran and Martin Sorenson and the others had suffered.

Bodie nodded to the manuscript in its scattered pages around the room.

'Read your way through that lot – and you'll find the name of your Banker.'

'No need for that.' Cowley was back to being chief of C.I.5, a grim, tough, dedicated man accustomed to scenes like this, with dead men and blood and terrified girls. This was just another facet of real life, a part of real life that – thankfully – was unknown to the majority of his fellow citizens.

'He'll not be far away. He'd want to get his hands on it

as quickly as possible. He wouldn't risk O'Leary carrying it half-way around London.' And then a change came over Cowley. It was not assumed. He did not have to pretend as he crossed to Helen Pierce. He could empathise with what she had gone through and his voice gentled and his face expressed the very real concern he felt.

'Miss Pierce ...'

'Yes?' Her colour still had not come back, and her stomach still felt as though it was trying to flutter out through her mouth. Everything had a blur around the edges. She felt sick. She was shaking, and seeing herself shake, and she could not stop that trembling, not stop it at all.

'Yes ...' She took a breath, gulping in the air with the acrid smell of gunsmoke. There was another, rawer smell, too, something like a not-too clean butcher's shop ...

'You've had a bad time,' Cowley was saying.

'Where's my father?'

Cowley took a breath. He regarded her soberly. 'I don't know. Not for sure. I can make a guess – but that's all it would be.'

'He's very ill.' Helen was appealing to them now, frightened afresh, and not for herself. 'He's dying –'

'Yes. I'm aware of that.'

'Look – all he wanted –'

'I know exactly what he wanted. But we'll get to that soon enough.' Cowley smiled at her, unforced, a genuine smile that calmed her a little. 'In the meantime –'

'He's paid for all he's done. He –'

Very firmly, Cowley continued. 'In the meantime there's something I must know, Miss Pierce. It's desperately important, believe me. Did he make a phone call – after he found the manuscript?' As Helen gazed blankly at him, Cowley went on: 'Did O'Leary make a phone call?'

'I – I can't remember.'

Now Cowley was very close to her, encouraging her, smiling, and going to lose the smile any minute under the urgency of the moment.

'Try. Try hard – please.'

'He said,' and she swallowed and put a shaking hand to her hair. 'He said – he'd got it.'

'Yes?'

'And – whoever it was he was talking to – should come and get it. He'd meet him in the street – yes – ' Her face screwed up and her eyes looked lost. 'I can't remember any more.'

'That's enough!' Cowley rose, looking relieved and – in the eyes of Bodie and Doyle – looking delighted. 'The Banker's no more than a stone's throw away – waiting for O'Leary to deliver the manuscript into his hands.' He bustled them to the door, not limping, brisk and business-like. 'We're looking for a big, expensive car – with a V.I.P. sitting in the back of it.'

As they clattered down the dingy stairs Cowley realised this was not a case of a breathless interest in *who* it was. It was one of those men whose faces had shown in old black and white photographs on the screen in Brigadier Stadden's study. No, this was a case of *catching* the man, never mind who he might be.

The car was spotted in a quiet side street, and it was just as Cowley had predicted, a big, black, shiny Daimler. The upholstery was real leather. The glass and paintwork shone. There was money there. The elegantly dressed man in the back fiddled with his suede gloves, impatiently waiting.

The passenger door opened and he looked up, startled, as Lewis slid in, to crowd him on the wide comfortable seat.

About to blast his anger at this intrusion, the man swung the other way as the other door opened and Cowley put his head in. He was not smiling. This man was being caught not just because of what he had done twenty years or more ago – the man was still at it, still the paymaster for a new ring; at least, that would be a sensible conclusion.

'The Right Honourable Paul Cantwell,' said Cowley. 'I believe. I have a message for you from Liam O'Leary. I'm afraid he can't make it. Neither can Pietro Callinari.'

Cantwell's full-fleshed features, twenty years older than those flashed up on the screen, tightened and then relaxed. It was difficult to believe this was happening – at last, and after so long.

Cowley went remorselessly on. 'They can't make it – they're otherwise detained. Don't worry, though. The manuscript is safe. I have it.' Cowley nodded his head to Lewis. 'All right. You know where to take him.' Cowley returned his attention to Cantwell. He spoke in such a way that Cantwell felt the words as blows across the face. 'Sorry I can't come with you, sir. I have to go and look for Thomas Darby.'

Cantwell panicked, then, as Cowley withdrew his head. He tried to make a bolt for it, and Lewis's very large and very capable hand closed on his arm. Firmly, Lewis shook his head. There was a one-way ticket waiting for the Right Honourable Paul Cantwell – Banker to spies.

When the man opened the door to Cowley it was possible for an unobservant person to mistake him for a servant. Cowley saw the broken nose, the way he walked, stiffly, as though something inside him had been broken a long time ago. Say, twenty years ago.

They were all sitting there, in the comfortable chairs, sitting quietly in Brigadier Stadden's book-lined and ochre-golden study. Stadden, himself, sat in his wheelchair with the plaid rug over his knees, and his beak-nosed face looked larger than life.

Cowley looked around at the others. Sorenson was there, grey and hunched and griped with pain. Elsa Coran sat, a frail bird-like woman, with eyes filled with ancient hate. The others were there, these survivors, these members of the club founded by Thomas Darby.

At the centre, in a large armchair, slumped the form of Darby. He was there, at the centre of his club. There were seven or eight people, all in their fifties or sixties, all grey and lined of face – and all marked by the same stigmas that set them apart, chained in bitter memories.

Darby did not move. His heavy doughy face relaxed, he sat there, and his head lolled.

Sorenson, Stadden, all of them, stared at Darby. They did not move their eyes as Cowley approached.

Sorenson said: 'We didn't kill him, Cowley.'

'His heart,' said Stadden.

'You would have killed him.'

Stadden coughed his words, stumbling, speaking as though he chewed grapes. 'I don't know. I suppose we intended to. But he was such a pathetic wreck . . . '

'And it all happened a long time ago?'

Even as he spoke Cowley realised what a damn fool remark that was. Time does not heal pain; the years do not make remembered agony any the sweeter.

Stadden simply said: 'Ask Sorenson. Or Elsa. Or any of the others.'

'No,' said Cowley. 'Twenty years – I'll have him taken away.'

'Thank you.' Stadden accepted this service as it was intended.

'No need for me to ask for your silence.'

'None at all,' said Stadden.

Cowley nodded. They all sat there, staring at Darby. He turned away and just before he reached the door, looking forward to escaping from the claustrophobic atmosphere of ancient evils, of the stirrings of old dust, Stadden spoke.

'Was there a manuscript, Cowley?'

'Yes.'

'Where is it?'

Cowley put his hand on the doorknob. 'Where do you think?'

Stadden's heavy voice rumbled like distant thunder in the dim library. 'No point in asking if I could read it?'

'None at all.'

Cowley opened the door. Stadden gave his heavy, hoarse, barking laugh, half a chuckle, half a groan of all the wasted years. 'Makes you a very powerful man, Cowley. Guardian of a thousand secrets.' And there was unmistakable mockery in the words and tones. What did these people care about the secrets of the future?

Cowley thought he should introduce a note of asperity into these ancient stirrings of dust. Briskly, he said:

'Aye. And don't you forget it, Brigadier.'

Then he went out.

The ancient dust had only a few more weary gyrations to make before it could sink back to rest.

The deserted and narrow road between the abandoned warehouses looked just the same. Yashinkov and his two aides got out of their big black limousine and, after the prescribed check, walked up to the second storey. Lewis switched on his cassette tape-recorder and hooked in his walkie-talkie. Yashinkov walked slowly forward along the dusty floor between the oblongs of yellow sunlight to the end, where Cowley, brooding, waited for him, with Bodie and Doyle in the shadows flanking him.

It was all the same as before – save for one thing.

In front of Cowley and resting on trestles lay a wooden box. The box was some six feet long, by two by two. It was made of plain yellow pine. But it exuded a sense of being other than it seemed.

Yashinkov halted, facing Cowley, and neither man smiled.

'Hello, comrade.'

'Hello, tovarich.'

'A lot has happened since we last met.'

Yashinkov nodded solidly. 'It would seem so.'

'There is the body of a dead man in that box.'

'Comrade Thomas Darby, perhaps.'

'Yes.' Cowley was firm. 'There is no record of his visit to London.'

'Good.'

'If you can get him back, unseen, to Moscow –'

'It can be arranged.' Yashinkov was already working on the best – and least inconvenient – method. But his face showed no trace of expression. 'The news of Comrade Colonel Thomas Darby's death –'

' – will be released sometime next week by *Pravda*.'

'I imagine so.' Now an icy smile crossed the K.G.B. man's square features. 'I think you will find he died next Monday.'

'I look forward to reading his obituary.'

Yashinkov spoke casually, as though wishing to clear up a minor point.

'Were there any – documents, papers . . .'

Bodie and Doyle stood, looking on, standing easily and yet ready for anything the Ivans might try to pull. Bodie was thinking of what all this meant in terms of anguish and suffering to Helen Pierce. Doyle was thinking that Helen Pierce would come out of it all O.K. She'd have help. He'd see to that.

Cowley spoke curtly.

'None.'

Yashinkov ducked his head in a little gesture that spoke volumes.

'I understand.'

'I,' said Cowley, 'hope so, Grigor.'

'Is there any more business?' The K.G.B. Controller's voice indicated a colder approach.

'Yes. I am delivering someone to your Embassy tomorrow morning. A passenger for the next available Aeroflot flight to Moscow.'

'Who is it?'

Cowley relished the words.

'Comrade the Right Honourable Paul Cantwell.'

The scowl that crossed Yashinkov's face made Bodie's nose twitch up, and gave Doyle a little recompense for the spot of bother they'd gone through.

'Ah,' said Yashinkov, taking refuge in the meaningless syllable.

'He is never,' Cowley told the Russian, 'to return to the United Kingdom.'

'Very well.'

'I must warn you. He's not very keen on going.' As

Yashinkov made no comment, Cowley continued. 'But I am sure you will make him feel comfortable and at home.'

Bleakly, Yashinkov said: 'They tell me the food has improved somewhat over the years in Lubianka.'

A thought struck him and the scowl vanished, to be replaced by a chilling smile.

'One day, tovarich, you must come over and try it.'

Doyle and Bodie let small delighted smiles show at this, behind George Cowley's broad back.

'I doubt if I'll get the opportunity, Grigor.'

'Pity.' It was clear to them all that Yashinkov meant that, meant it most profoundly: Then: 'Is that all?'

'Yes.'

The farewell procedure was gone through again with its echoes of dead leaves blowing in a dusty wind, and the Gate and the Checkpoint, and the dark limousines and the hidden guns. The aides stepped up to Bodie and Doyle.

As Doyle shook hands, he said: 'We'll ram your bloody car next time.'

Bodie shook hands with his opposite number.

'Up the Moscow Dynamos.'

The solemn reply came: 'Da.'

They stepped back. The shadows pressed down, the cobwebs hung in the corners, the dust strewed thickly over the floor.

Yashinkov nodded. 'Until the next time, tovarich.'

Cowley, Bodie and Doyle turned – not quite in unison – and walked away. This time they went, leaving the abandoned warehouse to the Russians. They stood, quietly, and the long pinewood box with all that was mortal of Thomas Darby lay quietly before them.

Going down the stairs Cowley reflected that it was no good dwelling on what had happened. They would be up to their necks in it soon, almighty soon if the last teleprinter printout about Mad Jack Rose was anything to go by. But that was for tomorrow.

C.I.5 – the Action Squad, the Big A – would go on, as it must go on whilst villainy still persisted. C.I.5 lived in the real world. The Professionals inhabited their own world and if in that world men died and women wept, didn't that make it just as much a real world as any other? The dust had lifted, just a little, and ghosts had walked – and now they must be about their business, ready to face in their own idiosyncratic way whatever the future might bring.

Bodie halted. His head went up and his eyes closed.

Doyle looked at him.

Bodie sneezed. He sneezed a ripe snorter. Then he looked apologetically at Cowley and Doyle.

'Dust,' said Bodie. 'Gets right up my hooter.'

Also in the PROFESSIONALS series:

THE PROFESSIONALS 5: BLIND RUN

by Ken Blake

C15 . . .

Society's tough answer to the spreading cancer of violence. A hand-picked, superbly-armed squad whose job is to get results in the relentless fight against crime and subversion.

Together, Doyle and Bodie are the spearhead of C15, the men they call the Professionals. And they're heading for trouble. Because trouble is their business . . .

BLIND RUN is the fifth fast-moving novel of action and suspense based on the adventures of London Weekend Television's THE PROFESSIONALS.

TV TIE-IN 0 7221 1728 0 85p

And don't miss the other adventures of THE PROFESSIONALS:

WHERE THE JUNGLE ENDS	85p
LONG SHOT	85p
STAKE OUT	85p
HUNTER HUNTED	85p

And selected from Sphere's Fiction lists

THE ROSS FORGERY

by William H. Hallahan

FORGED IN BLOOD ...

A ruthless millionaire with a complete – and very valuable – collection of *forged* first editions . . . another tycoon bent on revenge . . . and a type designer who'll do anything for the money he needs to buy himself creative freedom: these are the main characters in William H. Hallahan's stunning, suspense-packed novel of literary counterfeits and deadly human passions.

THE ROSS FORGERY is a compelling story of an attempt to create the perfect forgery – and a stark, powerful revelation of the more deadly forgery in men's hearts and minds . . .

'Ingenious . . . a twisting shocker of a conclusion . . . you wouldn't believe so much suspense and tension could be generated' *Washington Post*

PARADISE ONE

by Alan Harrington

YOU *MUST* LIVE FOR EVER

The year is A.D. 2007. The miraculous has occurred, for immortality has become a reality. And once achieved, a society without death should be serene, for its citizens have no shortage of time, no responsibilities, they have for ever to be themselves. Citizens of the Immortalist society enjoy programmed reincarnations – with compulsory years of sleep in between – in which they are free to act out their wildest dream-fantasies. So why should the governors of the Immortalist state become ever more autocratic? Why should they seek to erase the memories of dissenters? And who are the Death Partisans who assault Paradise?

'A sophisticated foray into the future . . . fascinating peeps at a human horror show' *Publishers Weekly*

GENERAL FICTION 0 7221 4419 9 £1.50